MW01592315

The Greatest Hijack

By Caroline Omoifo Ilogienboh

The Greatest Hijack

Cover background designed by Dianecostanzastudio

Except for the biblical references, all characters in this book have no existence except in the author's imagination. All biblical citations by characters in this book are indicated in the reference page.
Agba and Ologne villages are this author's creation.
The issues presented in this book are real and true to life.
Though the characters are fictional, extensive research and interviews were conducted to weave the storylines.

Some contents in this book are graphic and may not be suitable for young readers.

Printed in the United States by Morris Publishing®
3212 East Highway 30 • Kearney, NE 68847
1-800-650-7888

Acknowledgments

Years ago, my friend, Amife told me that as a young man he unmasked a masqueraded man who wounded a girl in my village, the place of my birth in Edo State, Nigeria. Unmasking a masquerade was considered a dishonor in the society, yet he defied the societal norm to protect the girl. I was filled with admiration for his courage. Little did I know that he planted a seed that would later be the foundation for the crafting of this book. My village practiced female circumcision at that time.

Over the years, my friend's altruistic disposition allowed me to observe a man's protective nature when charged with saving others who are at risk. Lessons learned from him were used to model some of the male characters in this book.

The crossing of our paths was not an accident.

Amife, ebullient son of Esanland, brave son of Esan people, as you unmasked a girl's adversary in a small village in Nigeria, you have greatly helped in unmasking the culprit behind the wounding of millions of women and girls worldwide.

Om'ojie, obulu, many thanks. You're simply the best of friends.

Special thanks to:

Joshua Imonmion, you were on-call, ready to research any subject matter I sent to you. Your wealth of information was a great asset. May you be mightily rewarded.

Dorothy Howell, our love for creating better lives for young ladies brought us together. My dear sister in Christ, like a nurse who cuts the umbilical cord of a new baby, you took on this book, cleaning it up.

My friends, Kristen Carrotto and Mary Gayle Scheper, you two have the patience of saints. You never tire of listening to the ideas that come out of my restless brain. Our morning walks are precious gifts.

My friend, Violet Iluebbey and I migrated to America not knowing what the future held for us. We have gone through the valleys and the mountains and by the grace of God, we're still standing. Thank you for checking up on me every night when I locked myself down to write this book.

Ellen Sudderth of ESP book chats, the spirit of God sent you to search for me. Three years search, you finally found me to talk about my book, Saving Bekyah. Questions raised during the interview led to the writing of this book. May the Holy Spirit continue to use you to encourage writers and seekers.

Anna Miranda, Patience Olotu, Agnes Malgapo, Omotayo Amedu, and Mrs. Rose Abba, your prayers are lifelines. Thank you.

My children, Ebinehita, Ofure, and Osenemedia, and my young friends, Isimenmen Olotu and Ere Ehiaghe, may you continue to blossom.

Jason Luke, Linda Luke, Sonala Olumhense, George Enabosi, Matt Pizzano, Nick Carrotto, Pamela Chiariello, Jide Fawole, Rose Ilogienboh, and Beth Karper, much appreciation for your friendship.

Rejoice Anthony, our Sunday talks and prayers are always heart-warming.

My sister, Dr. Professor Juliana Okoh, I'm glad to follow in your footsteps in advocating for the welfare of women.

My brother-in-law, Dr. Professor J.D. Okoh, our thought-provoking talks during the 2020 COVID lockdown at Ubiaja, Edo State, kept my mind alive. I was thrilled the day you called me a 'Jesus' fanatic'.

My church family at St. Raphael Parish, Livingston, New Jersey, I cherish your encouragement. God bless you all.

Rev. Fr. Jose Erlito Ebron, thank you for listening to my chatter about this book. Our talks were very enlightening.

And Prince Amos Enabosi, I'm grateful for the gift of your presence.

In The Beginning

The breadth and depth of heaven illuminated with a warm glow. Multiple displays of light sparked, showing the glory of God. The angels blew trumpets in jubilation. There was a great rumbling of joy to announce the creation of man. His name is Adam.

They placed the new man in the garden of Eden. The Lord God instructed him to eat out of every tree in the garden except one. He must not eat out of the tree of knowledge of good and evil, he will die if he eats from the tree.

The man named every beast of the field, every bird of the sky, and every living creature that was brought to him. Yet none was a suitable companion.

Then God put him into a deep sleep. While the man slept, God opened his flesh, took one of his ribs, and closed the place with flesh. Then God formed a woman out of the rib that was taken from the side of man. God awakened him and presented the woman to him.

Filled with joy, the man proclaimed, "This is bone of my bone, and flesh of my flesh." He called her Eve, for she would be the mother of all.

The man shall leave his father and his mother and join with his wife, and the two become one flesh. They were both naked and were not ashamed.

And so began humanity in creating Adam and Eve.

(Adapted from the Holy Bible, Contemporary English Version)

Chapter 1

Agba, Nigeria

"Khi!" Malina Danishe screamed, saliva flew out of her mouth. She wiped her lips with the back of her hand as she swirled with her eyes, searching. The fly zoomed past her again. She slowly leaned towards the table to grab a plate, keeping her gaze steady on the offender. Leaping up, she scooped the fly, burying it under the plate. She slammed the plate face down on the table. "Ah-ha! choro, I got you." So sure that she caught it, she breathed a sigh of relief. Like a deflated balloon, her chest fell when she lifted the plate and a space gaped at her. She cursed with such venom that if the fly had been human, it would have fought back. The fly was not the actual cause of her anger; what they did to her enraged her.

The sight of her bloodied, discarded clothes on the floor only brought her more grief. Closing her eyes, she shut them tightly and prayed not to remember. It was no use. The battered flesh between her legs burned. Slowly sliding on the floor, she used her hands to cover her face.

How can they do something so painful to prepare for marriage? She couldn't understand. She pleaded with her stepmother not to allow it, but her stepmother insisted it was tradition. They must circumcise every girl before marriage. No marriage for her, she told her parents. That was not an option, they informed her. They forced it on her two weeks ago. She has refused to leave her room since the procedure.

Marriage proposals were on the table. Malina hoped her parents would respect her wish not to be married. She heard a sound coming from outside the walls of their high-fenced house. It was a sign that something ceremonious was about to happen. Her heartbeat pulsated, she took a deep breath and let the torrent of tears flow out of her eyes.

The household of Mr. Bani Danishe has never seen such a large group of audience. He was extremely proud that his compound was big enough to accommodate the crowd. Delight filled him up. His beautiful 20-year-old daughter, Malina, has commanded an affluent suitor. It impressed him that Ayoni Johnan presented two cows as a dowry for his daughter's hand in marriage. He preferred this young man to the one that came the year before. He tried to remember the man's name; it escaped his memory. The annoying man hadn't the common sense to bring him a goat to slaughter. The information he gathered about the previous suitor showed he recently opened a provision store that wasn't doing well. His father was scurrying around for some money to buy the seven cows that were required by tradition to get married.

Mr. Danishe grinned. Ayoni was the suitable man for his daughter. The dilemma he faced was his daughter didn't want to marry. It saddened him that the money he used in training Malina in higher education would go to waste. He didn't provide her an education to sit at home. Ayoni would give him a good compensation for his daughter and provide for her as well. It would be a shame to let all these go since she certainly couldn't discern the difference between a future of living in poverty to a life of luxury. No, he wouldn't let that happen. She must marry Ayoni.

He looked at the crowd; they looked on like spectators at a festival who had no intention of missing a piece of the entertainment. He braced himself to welcome the visitors.

Dum, dum, the drums drowned the chatting voices. It was time for the suitor to present his proposal. Ayoni, accompanied by several men gregariously dressed in African garbs, stepped forward. He signaled to a servant, and a herd of cows wandered into the yard. Afraid of being thumped, people stepped back to give way to the herd. Ayoni raised his hand, and the herdsman guided the cows back out of the yard. The cows' breasts were soggy, showing they weren't milked in weeks; another sign that Ayoni was affluent enough to let go of the money each cow could have brought in. As if on cue, the crowd gathered back as soon as the herd retreated from the yard.

"Many greetings to the Honorable Mr. Danishe," Ayoni spoke loudly. "And greetings to all!" Applaud rang out among the crowd. Ayoni beamed from ear to ear, he raised his hand to silence the crowd. He stepped to the podium and announced his intention for the beautiful Malina. "No one in this land has produced such beauty as the Honorable Danishe. Today, before you all, I declare my intention to make Malina my wife."

Mr. Danishe clapped his hands. "Well done, my son," he said proudly. He approached Ayoni. He hugged the younger man, and then turned to the people, nodding his approval. The crowd cheered. He turned to the servant. "Bring my daughter."

Malina sneaked a peek at the courtyard. She saw the red scarf and her heartbeat dropped. She has held her breath, praying that when she looked out of the window, she'd see the white scarf. Now she knew it was up to her to save herself from being hurled off to Ayoni's estate. She leaped on her feet at the slight knock on the door; she expected it. Her maid, Abie, rushed in, dropped the scarves, and packed things into a suitcase. Abie skirted around, picking up items discarded by Malina. "Sorry," she said, without meeting Malina's gaze. "I prayed that the red scarf wouldn't come up. It took me a lot of strength to lift it up."

"That's okay," Malina said absent-mindedly. "It wasn't your fault. I knew it was going to be one or the other. Red if my father accepts Ayoni's proposal and white if he declines. I suspected my father would go for Ayoni's proposal but hoped he wouldn't. Now I know what I must do." She changed into a pair of jeans, dropped her fancy dress on the floor, and swept her hair into a bun. "Are you ready?" she asked Abie.

"Yes."

"Are you sure about this? You'd get into trouble."

"I couldn't let you wander into the unknown alone," Abie said with compassion. "I swore to your mother that I'd forever be with you."

"Thank you."

4

With as much possession as they could carry, the two women sneaked out of the house. Malina glanced at her father's compound. She shook her head regrettably. No one will make her marry. Her father could find her when he got that message.

They had walked a mile when Malina heard tires screeching on the unpaved road. She grabbed Abie's hand, leading her into the bush. "Shh, shh," she whispered. They remained still. So sure, that the vehicle had passed by, she signaled Abie to come behind her out of their hideout. It completely took her aback when powerful hands curled around her mouth and another around her waist. Swept off the ground, they threw her into a truck. Abie met the same fate. Their eyes were covered with a piece of cloth, and soon the truck zoomed off to an unknown destination. They kidnapped them. By whom she didn't know, and she was afraid to ask. Could it be her father? Her heartbeat throbbed joyously for a moment, and then the other possibility creeped in. Her heartbeat plummeted as fast as it had lifted with the earlier joy.

After being bounced up and down on some rugged roads, the car came to a stop. They ushered them out and led them to another destination. Malina wanted to protest but knew the hand that held her was fierce. She'd wait until she got to wherever they headed. They pushed her in and untied her. Her eyes took a few minutes to adjust. It was a bedroom, stylish and plush. Whose room, was it? She didn't wonder for long. Her heart skipped a beat when he walked in. Her inner alarm sounded, warning her she was in danger. She looked left and right. The room had one door, and he was standing in front of it. With a devilish look, he came towards her.

Chapter 2

Lagos, Nigeria

Babza Tabor, CEO of Tabor Advertising Company, shook hands with the last recipient. He congratulated those who received this year's excellence and achievement award. The fifty team members applauded. When it died down, he began his annual speech.

"Ladies and gentlemen, not everyone made it to the awards list. This doesn't mean that you're valued less. In a growing organization like ours, there is room for growth. I urge you to bring forth your very best foot. The goals of this company are not changeable, but your tactics for accomplishing them are. I encourage you to network with other agencies. I suggest you seek ideas from professionals like yourself; you can be creative."

A staff member raised her hand. Babza paused, and then asked her to speak.

"I'm often discouraged when I tell people my idea and they discount it," Josephine Ihden said.

"That's common," Babza replied lightly. "It's important that when communicating your idea to ask this question, who can kill it? Get the person on board, seek others and get them in."

Another staff member, Greg Igbokwe stated, "I have presented several ideas, and no one bought into them."

Babza acknowledged his concern by looking directly at him. "As much as I encourage your ideas, you should first ask this, does the purpose of my idea align with the company's mission. There's no point in churning out ideas that we can't use." He looked around, expecting more hands or a puzzled look. He didn't see any. "You would agree that all the wise men and all the wise men's horses should head in the same direction. I encourage innovative ideas on how best we can get the job done. Ask yourself this, why do I do what I do and why does it matter? Can you explain what we do to others? The more you know what you do and why, the more confidence you build in yourself, and others would have in you."

He looked at their faces. They were attentive. "You're expected to come to work and perform. We give you our current data. Use it to decide your options. The trend shows a good outcome, but we can kick it up a notch. Not doing it is like getting on your treadmill and putting it on level one. You might as well read your newspaper or drink your coffee instead of pretending to be exercising. Don't fool yourself, set a higher standard and break out in a sweat." He lowered his voice, "You're the ones in the trenches; bring back ideas as they occur. If in doubt, ask. No one would withhold food from you if you don't have the right view."

His cell phone rang, interrupting him. He glanced at it; the caller was his friend, Kayah. He'd call him later. He put the phone on silent.

"Don't keep people in the dark," he continued. "Make it a habit to tell your clients what happens next. Answer their questions as honestly as you can. If you fill people with nonsense and suddenly want their cooperation, their response may shock you, and that may be because they don't trust you. Keep your appointments; you would get more cooperation from a horse with his head under your canopy than one at a distance. Remember that a satisfied customer tells 2 people, an unsatisfied customer tells 20. Are you all following me?" he asked.

"Yes, sir," they responded

"Good. This brings me to the next item, documentation. Record keeping is part of your functions. A job well done is not complete until you have put it in writing where someone else can see it. All pertinent client information needs to be written. What if you were in a hospital and you're allergic to penicillin, wouldn't you want it in your chart? Same here, every paper affects someone's life. I want to know a client's full history when I pick up a folder. I want to know what action plan or strategy you have put in place to combat any problem." He pointed a finger and added, "Your integrity is on the line." In closing, he announced, "It's lunchtime, have fun."

The group got on their feet. Babza excused himself, rushing to his office. On his desk was a note to call Kayah. He wondered what was amiss. He quickly dialed his number. "I got your message," he said to Kayah when he came on the line.

"Thanks for calling back," Kayah uttered anxiously.

"What's wrong?"

"My sister is missing."

"Missing?"

"Yes, my father said a suitor came to the house to ask for her hand in marriage. Malina disappeared."

"Oh, she probably doesn't want the man. I'm sure she'd surface when the suitor leaves."

"There's more. I'm worried about her state of mind."

"Give me the entire story."

"My younger brother said two weeks ago, they whisked Malina away and when she came back, she had blood on her clothes. She was screaming and cursing from here to heaven. He even said some men held her down from going completely crazy. She was in hysteria."

"What happened to her?"

"They took her for circumcision."

"OMG! They still do that in your place?"

"This is all news to me. I don't know what to do. I called you because you know about this from the reform that happened in your village some years ago."

"I only helped a bit. The person who stopped them was Candice. She went back to the US."

"I'm very upset about this," Kayah said dejectedly.

"Let's find your sister first. I'll meet with you this evening."

"Okay, thanks."

After ending the conversation, Babza moved to gaze out of his office window. Female circumcision, he knew how hard Candice fought in his village to end the procedure. He had supported her; he didn't believe any female should go through it, but people hold tight to their tradition.

His encounter with a female in this category was a challenging experience. He paused, thinking of the woman. She was beautiful by all standards. He had

10

impatiently sought her out; sent her love notes, jewelry, and entertained her with candlelight dinners at the best restaurants in Lagos. It excited him when she finally agreed to his overtures.

The minute she walked into his house; he couldn't hold down his arousal to mate with her. He wasted no time in taking her to bed. He slipped his fingers inside her panties, stroking and feeling her. His fingers froze when he noticed something was missing. The upper part of her vulva was scraped. He removed his fingers from that part, concentrating on other parts instead. He got disconcerted when they engaged, and he found her dry. After a few minutes of love making, he feared he was hurting her. He wasn't a narcissist, not to be concerned. Even though she assured him she was fine, he couldn't deal with the nagging feeling that she wasn't enjoying his love making as she wanted him to believe. With that uncertainty looming over his passion, it dampened his interest to continue the engagement. He knew that if he could have stimulated her missing hood, she'd get an out-pour of her natural lubricant. That hadn't been an option. His excitement died, and he disengaged.

Coming out of reverie, he was at a point of not dating for fear of running into one of them. His onetime encounter was enough. Sighing deeply, he wondered how long this issue would continue to plague his world. And who the hell started it all? His head felt heavy. The subject often brought him an onslaught of migraine headaches. He felt unusually warm. He loosened the tie around his neck. Even though his office was spacious, it felt like the walls were closing upon him. He opened the window and laid his back on the couch. His eyelids slowly closed.

Chapter 3

The Grand Tour

Babza fell into a deep sleep. An angel of the Lord pried his eyes open. Bright lights beamed into his eyeballs. He blinked, then looked through the light. The lenses behind the iris and pupil adjusted, exposing his vision to beyond the light.

A deep voice beckoned him to come up. He leaned forward. The voice sounded familiar, like that of his grandfather. He obeyed and followed.

He wasn't sure if he walked on solid ground, his feet compelled him to keep moving.

"Don't be afraid," the Voice said. "You're going on a tour." When no response came from Babza, the Voice prompted him. "It's okay to speak, son."

Babza suddenly felt highly energetic, the kind he used to feel when he was a teenage boy; always filled with bountiful curiosity. "Where is this place?" He didn't wait for an answer, he stepped into the unknown.

The ambiance was filled with an explosion of colors of different hues, iridescent pink enmeshed in blue, red, yellow, and white dancing flirtatiously with each other. Trees bloomed with lush green leaves. A light breeze brushed the leaves, they swayed in perfect union with the atmosphere. Water trickled over stones before gently flowing into a large stream. Subtle underwater lighting shimmered in it. Chirping sounds of birds and their flapping wings tickled his ears. A delightful fragrance drifted into his nostril. He inhaled deeply and then bounced off like Tarzan in a quest to discover the next attractive tree to climb.

"Slow down, son," the Voice told him.

Babza collected himself, "Sorry, it's magnificent here."

"I know. I live here. Beyond this place is God's exquisite abode."

"Do I get to meet God?" he asked excitedly.

"No, son."

"Okay, how about Jesus?"

"No, but he brought you here for a history lesson."

"History!" Babza yelped. "I could get that from the newspaper or internet. This place is too grand for me to learn anything."

"Ah! We noticed your sharp acumen. You built a successful business from nothing, and you can talk the most dejected person into feeling good about themselves."

"I guess you're right," Babza concurred.

"Of course, I'm right. Jesus knew you from your mother's womb. You bear the name of one of his relatives."

"Really? I thought my name was different. I have wondered why my parents picked it." He pondered that for a second. "You can call me Babu. That was my nickname when I was young. I think it matches how I feel right now."

"Okay, Babu. Let's begin."

Like a spectator in a stage play, Babu settled down to watch the scene as a curtain pulled back. He leaned closer.

The Voice said, "This is a celebration."

"It looks amazing," Babu remarked.

On display, angels floated about, and loud melodious music graced the stage. A bright, spectacular show of thunderbolts, lights, and fireworks displayed the glory of God. The angels played trumpets, harps, and horns in jubilation. All the choirs of angels, except one, sang holy, holy, holy. The curtain closed, and the Voice spoke to Babu.

"That festivity commemorated the creation of humans, Adam and Eve. The Lord God placed Adam in the garden of Eden and then formed the woman, Eve, to be with him. The holiest one announced that by grace, the humans would be higher than angels. Adam and Eve could eat every fruit from the various trees except one. The Lord forbid them to eat from the tree of knowledge of good and evil. Their disobedience will lead to death. They will enjoy all heavenly favors if they remain faithful to God. The man and the woman found delight in their home. Heavenly angels, except Satan, cheered them with joyous echoes which rang through the atmosphere.

"Why wasn't Satan happy like the others?" Babu asked.

"He didn't care about humans, particularly the last created creature, the woman."

"Why?"

"She was beautiful. He compared her to his own beauty. He felt insulted that human would rise above angels. Never, he said. He'd crush them."

"Can he?"

"Satan convinced himself that he had as much power as God. He eyed the humans contemptuously. He would

14

manipulate and disconnect them from God. Satan vowed to prove that humans were weak and inferior. He'd make sure they come under his rule and serve him. It would show that he was the ruler of the earth."

"Did he succeed?" Babu asked.

"Day and night, Satan observed Adam and Eve in the garden. He paid special attention to the woman. She looked delicate. She'd be much easier to manipulate, he concluded. He remembered Adam's delirious delight when God presented Eve to him. Adam proclaiming, 'bone of my bone, flesh of my flesh' annoyed Satan, but he saw an insight into Adam's heart. He loved his new partner. Satan knew that Adam's deep attachment to Eve would serve his purpose."

"So, what did he do?" curious Babu asked.

"Now among all the animals, the snake was the most cunny. Its structure was also very pliable. It could slither in and out quickly. Satan used the snake as a medium to tempt Eve. The snake came to the garden daily, hovering around the forbidden tree. It made sounds that made Eve smile. The snake lingered by the fruit, making it look more luscious and desirable than the rest of the fruit in the garden. It lured her and stirred her interest, pulling her closer to the tree. Satan was happy. He got the woman's attention and the means. He set the stage for his next move."

"This is interesting," Babu commented.

"Eve was alone in the garden when the serpent slithered to engage her in a conversation. It convinced her to eat the fruit. She took some of the fruit and ate it. Adam came back. She told him of her conversation with the serpent, and that she had eaten the forbidden fruit. She

15

gave some to Adam, and he also ate it. God found out that they had disobeyed him, he banished them from the garden."

"Whoa!" exclaimed Babu. "That serpent was a clever interloper."

"Yes, Babu. You're very perceptive," the Voice lightly commended his quick thinking. "Now, look to your far right."

Babu saw a curtain lift. He saw a man looking down but cocked his head as if listening to someone else.

"That's Abraham in a conversation with God. God told Abraham he will be a father to many descendants. God made a covenant with Abraham to circumcise himself and every male in his household. They shall circumcise the flesh of their foreskin in every generation. And any uncircumcised male shall be cut off from his people."

"Interesting," Babu observed.

"Look over there to your far left," the Voice said. "That is Sarah and Tobias. Sarah had married 7 husbands, and each died on their wedding night. Tobias is her eighth husband."

"What killed all the seven husbands?" Babu asked.

"Your lesson has ended," the Voice informed Babu. "Write them in your heart for there lies what you seek."

"I have one more question," Babu said quickly. "How do all these relate to each other?"

"The only thing I will share with you is what John wrote in the apocalypse's book, the dragon laid in wait for the pregnant woman to devour her child."

Babza felt hands shaking him. He slowly came awake. He opened his eyes and then jumped up.

His secretary, Toki, shifted backward with her mouth open. Her puzzled frown showed her confusion. "Sir," she said to get his attention when she found her voice. "Are you okay?"

"I don't know," Babza said in a muffled tone. "How long have I been asleep?"

"I'm not sure, sir. I've been trying to talk to you for the past ten minutes."

"Please leave me alone for a few minutes." He waived her off, dismissing her. He got a bottle of water from the refrigerator in the room and uncapped it. In one long gulp, he emptied the bottle. He sat back down to recall the vision.

Chapter 4

Brooklyn, New York, USA

"How was the party yesterday?"

"It was a beautiful night for a retirement celebration," Candice responded to her friend, Lorita. "The moon shimmered brightly. I arrived a bit early, so I could leave early. I nibbled on light refreshments, had some red wine, and chatted with old and new friends. It was a pleasant atmosphere for a Friday night."

"Please skip the preamble," Lorita said. She was eager to hear the gist of the encounter between Candice and her old boss, Kesson.

"Gallantry," Candice declared.

"Okay, what does that mean?"

"The only way to describe how he walked in. I didn't feel the usual loss of breath whenever I'm in his presence, which was good. I gave him eye contact, acknowledging his arrival. He settled by a table far from me, which was perfect since I didn't want to be in his direct line of vision. Later, he got up and strolled around the room, exchanging greetings with friends. I looked away as he neared my table. He touched my shoulder briefly. I acknowledged him with a slight nod, and he left."

Her recount enthralled Lorita, she wanted her to spill it out quickly. She knew Candice was dragging it out so she could relive the encounter. Lorita talked herself into calming down. She'd give her friend the room to enjoy the pleasure of her tale.

"After dinner, several people made speeches and farewells to the celebrant. I walked around the room, taking pictures with friends. I didn't know he was at my side until I felt his hand on my shoulder. He had left his seat to sandwich himself in between a colleague and me where we posed for a picture. We became a threesome with him in the middle."

"Nice," Lorita said dreamily.

"He returned to his seat afterward, and I returned to mine. Shortly after, I observed him walk to the restroom. Guessing he'd be coming out any moment, I walked to a spot where he'd be within earshot. Soon as he came out, I whispered that I had a dream in which he and I were in a compromising position. He smiled and said, 'I like that.' I went back to my seat. Across the room, I glimpsed his eyes on me. Our eyes met, and I looked away. It was time to leave, anyway. I said my goodbyes and headed towards the exit. He pulled my arm when I walked past him. He walked me to my car, and that was when we kissed."

"How was it?" Lorita asked enthusiastically.

"Heavenly. Kissing him always gives me a yummy feeling."

"Go on," Lorita prodded her.

"We were touching and feeling each other, and then…"

"What?"

"His live-in girlfriend appeared at the entrance of the restaurant, looking for him, I guess."

"She walked in on both of you?" Lorita said with a disappointing undertone.

"No, we cut it off. He left with her, and I drove home."

"I was just getting excited."

Candice didn't want to relive her frustration, anger or whatever ugly emotion went through her the moment their tryst ended. "Hmm, that's it," she said resignedly. She changed the subject. "Now let's talk about Janice Welsh."

"She's in the meditation room."

"That's good. She needs the quiet time to reflect on how to bring order to her life." Filled with pride, Candice said, "That's the purpose of setting up the Center for Women."

Later that night, Candice let out the turmoil in her emotion. She went into that lonesome road she accepts as part of her life. Daytime, she was a boisterous, confident, and assertive woman, but immersed in lonely misery at night. She had hoped that her meeting with Kesson would deliver her from the agony of loneliness. Unfortunately, that didn't happen.

She dragged herself to her bed and lay down. Why was her life so difficult? She thought of her dead mother who left her at a time she could barely walk. She wondered what her life would look like had her mother lived. Her grandmother, whom she lived with, raised her as if she were in the military. Everything was so regimented that she had no room to be a child. Her marriage to Sagha was nothing but an emotional assault. The relationship with Kesson didn't favor her. She lay her head on the pillow, looking up. A light flow of tears slid down her cheek. She let it meander down to her pillow. Sleep finally relieved her of her misery.

In her dream, she heard him call her name. No answer came from her. She didn't want to be disturbed, especially by a stranger. She sat on the floor with her arms wrapped around her bent legs. Her forehead lay between her knees. He called her again. Remaining mute, she looked up. Her vision didn't go past his middle. She could tell he was tall.

"I want to be left alone," she uttered slowly and then returned her head to its prior position.

"You can talk to me."

On one hand, she wanted to be left alone, but also wanted to talk to someone, even if it's a ghost. Taking him up on his offer, she asked, "Since you want to talk, can you tell me why my life is so hard?"

"Hard, huh."

"See, you don't even believe me." She shook her head. "In the middle of the night, I'm talking to a phantom. I'm definitely going crazy?"

"No, you're not."

"You don't even know me."

"I knew you from the day we formed you."

"And you knew it would be a miserable life."

"Yes."

"Since you were there, tall guy, why didn't you stop my conception before birth instead of having this conversation now."

"I couldn't," he said flatly. "You came for a reason."

"I did it. I saved Bekyah from circumcision."

"It is not finished."

She questioned why she's talking to a ghost. Dismissing him, she said, "I'm tired. Please leave me alone."

"There's more."

Candice hesitated briefly, and then asked, "Another Bekyah to save?"

"You won't understand now. It's bigger than Bekyah."

"Can't someone else do it?"

"You were faithful in one, you are now given more."

"I've heard that before, it's somewhere in the bible." She was thoughtful for a minute. "It was such a lonely road with so much opposition."

"Which you overcame."

"True. But..."

"We heard the cries of all our daughters. In saving Bekyah, we sent you ahead of one who will unveil the truth. Now, you must join him."

"A him? Does he know about this?"

"No, not yet anyway."

"I'm scared."

He laughed. "You, scared? No, not you."

"Yes, me. I'm human. I have feelings. When saving Bekyah, my people betrayed me, they turned against me and threatened to kill me. I have a right to be scared."

"I understand. My people did the same to me, too."

Candice suddenly knew the stranger may be... she stopped herself. She was hallucinating. Another thought gnawed at her. Did she die? Was she in heaven?"

As if reading her thoughts, he said, "You didn't die. You're in your bedroom."

Relieved, she sighed. "How would I know him?"

"You will get a sign."

"I don't know," she muttered cautiously. "This is frightening."

"Do not be afraid. I will be with you always."

22

"My head hurts so much." She massaged her forehead with her fingertips. "You were saying...?" She looked up; the tall man has disappeared. She suddenly became fully awake. The clock showed 3:15 am. Go back to sleep, she told herself. It was a dream. Come morning, she won't remember it. She buried herself under her covers and dozed off.

Chapter 5

Lagos, Nigeria

Kayah's doorbell chimed. He let Babza into the room. "We still haven't found her."

"You said she went with her maid."

"Yes."

"Any word on the maid?"

"No. Both families are meeting tonight. I'll head there first thing tomorrow morning."

"Has she done this before?"

"No. She was a very dedicated student. Her schoolwork was always her priority."

"Contact all her friends. I'm sure someone would know something."

"I told my younger brother to reach out to her best friend. He'd call me when he returns." Kayah paced the room. "This shouldn't be happening."

"You said she ran away because of the circumcision."

"I was told that my stepmother informed her it's our tradition to do the cutting before marriage. Malina blatantly refused to go through with it. She threatened that if they insist, she wouldn't marry. I guess they didn't take her seriously." Kayah went to the refrigerator in the

24

kitchen to get a bottle of water. He offered Babza a bottle of beer. "Against her wish, some men came to the house and whisked her off to where they did the procedure. My brother said she's been crying every day."

"It's unfortunate," Babza remarked glumly.

Kayah's face creased painfully. "Someone took a razor and cut up my baby sister in the most delicate part of her body. My inside is boiling. I'm going to kill those bastards when I get there tomorrow."

"I'd feel the same if I were in your shoes," Babza empathized.

"When I came back from Somalia some years ago, I asked my father if my town perform circumcision on females, and he said, no. He just informed me he meant they don't do it the same way as in Somalia."

"You've lost me," Babza uttered, looking puzzled.

"I went on an assignment for my newspaper in Somalia. An old roommate from my university in the UK got married when I was there. The wedding was impressive. I stayed with some other friends at a villa. Late on the wedding night, the groom came to the villa, looking ghastly. He was so upset that he vomited. Naturally, we got concerned. Thinking he had too much alcohol consumption, we got him comfortable. My host urged him to go back to his bride afterwards. My friend shook his head, his whole body bunched up in pain. The three of us in the room looked at each other, worried. We then suspected something was wrong with the marital bed. My host immediately knelt beside my friend, speaking in their language. He later told me that the groom froze when he saw the wife's vagina. The clitoris wasn't there, and they used threads to stitch the labia together. There was a pair of scissors on the bedside for him to cut the threads. He had picked up the scissors and his hand shook violently. He threw the scissors down and ran out of the room." Painful streaks formed across Kayah's face. "It was shocking to me. I didn't know things like that happened on this planet. I told my father when I came back home, and he said we don't do that here. He just told me he meant we don't do the stitching style or infibulation, as it's called. They cut the clitoris in my town."

Babza cringed. "This is so heart breaking."

"Jesus!" Kayah scowled. "Someone, like a butcher at a meat market, striped my sister naked, held her down, and cut off the flesh between her legs. Cold cut!" He bent over, groaning deeply. "I'm sick to my stomach."

Perturbed, Babza broke into a cold sweat. Beads of perspiration drifted down his spine. The horror was deeper than he was aware. He felt his friend's pain, his own chest constricted. "What should we do?" he asked.

"I don't know." He shook his head. "This shouldn't have happened. Had I known what my father meant, I would have intervened and spared my sister from this horror."

"Don't take the blame for this," Babza said soothingly.

Collecting himself, Kayah said, "I need to find my sister."

"I agree. Let me know how I can help."

Chapter 6

Lagos, Nigeria

Another busy day at work, Babza thought as he entered his house. Three business meetings in one day left him drained. He threw his briefcase on the side table and collapsed on the couch. His muscles relaxed. He suddenly jolted up. The vision crept into his conscious mind again. He has tried to push it into the back of his mind, but now and then it would resurface. Grabbing a piece of paper and a pen, he began to write.

Hours later, he stared at the things he had written. They made little sense to him. He was a Christian, but not a practicing one. He knew enough to know he could find these things in the bible, but he didn't own one. Should he see a pastor? No, he didn't belong to a church. They would call him crazy if he walked into any church and tell them how he received what he has written. Speaking on an unfamiliar subject often causes him unnecessary anxiety. He must do something, but at a loss on what to do. After several minutes of helplessness, he decided to visit his hometown. He'd talk with his father. He booked a flight.

New York, USA

Candice shifted her cell phone from one ear to the other. "Papa, you said you've had malaria for two weeks. Are you sure it's malaria?"

"This is not the first time I've had malaria. I know what it feels like," her father, the Osunih of Ologne village, responded.

"Did you get the COVID vaccine as I told you to do last time we spoke?"

"No," the Osunih replied. "I went to the health center. They said the supply didn't come from the government."

"Papa, I'm worried about you. Anyway, I called to let you know I'm coming home next week."

"Oh, my daughter, that would make me very happy. I haven't seen you in a long time."

"Me too, that's why I'm coming. It's been a long time."

"Alright then. This time I will get to spend plenty of time with you. No saving Bekyah like the last time."

"Yes, papa. We will spend time together."

"Amah, daughter of Ogbodu, the gbedeke of Ologne land. We will welcome you home."

"Thank you, papa. Bye for now."

A bright smile lit her face after she hung up. She'd love to be in her village. Managing the women's center has kept her so busy that she forgot the thrill of being in her quiet village in Nigeria. It would be nice to savor the pleasure of stepping away from the hustle and bustle of New York. This morning, she felt an urgent longing to see her father. She hated to dismiss her instinct when it nudges her to do something. Her experience has taught her never to ignore her inner voice. She was happy she bought the ticket to Nigeria.

Chapter 7

Malina was panic-stricken. She stood rigid as if embalmed in a standing position. He touched her. His fingers felt like live electric wires; the shock jump-started her immobile body. She jetted away from him. "Don't touch me!" she screamed.

Ayoni emitted a devilish laugh. "Your father approved my marriage proposal. You shouldn't have escaped. You embarrassed me when you didn't show up yesterday."

Was she supposed to feel sorry for him? Malina questioned silently. She had expressed her desire not to marry to her father and Ayoni. The two seemed to think her opinion didn't count. "I don't want to marry. Not before, not now or ever."

The rejection seared through him like a poisonous snakebite. Something unleashed inside him. In one swift movement, he pulled her to himself. "Don't you ever repeat those words," he snapped at her. "I will marry you."

She felt the pressure of his hand on her arm. She struggled to dislodge his hold. "Leave me!" The weight of his hand on her became painful. Malina refused to cower; she wouldn't give him that satisfaction. She must get away from him. Her eyes scanned the room, looking for an escape outlet.

He bellowed, "Don't even think of it. My guards and dogs will hunt you down."

Malina pushed him, ran past him, gunning for the door. She was no match for his strides. He was upon her before she reached the door. They both landed on the floor. She scrambled from under him, rising to run away. He grabbed her foot, pulling her. She fought back with as much energy as she could muster. Taking a wooden stool from the corner, she smashed it on his head and ran out of the room.

He yelped, "Yeh! What is wrong with you?" He got up and ran after her. He caught up with her in the long hallway and dragged her back into the room.

Undeterred, she hit him in his stomach. That seemed to put him in a daze.

Her eyes caught the open window, she dashed for it. She grabbed the window frame, pulling her whole body up. Balancing her feet, she looked down. The ground was hundreds of feet below her. She would jump to her death.

"Stop, don't jump!" he screamed.

"I want to die," she cried out.

"Please come down. You don't have to marry me."

"It's not you. I told my father I don't want to be cut. They did it anyway. I have no value, so why live?"

He breathed a sigh of relief. "That is why you ran away? Come down."

"Didn't you hear me? They did this to me because of marriage. I'm scarred for life. I'll kill myself."

"You're beautiful, let's talk about it." He slowly crept up towards her.

"No!" She removed her hands from the window, lifting her feet to jump.

With the agility of a trained soldier, he sprang and quickly grabbed her legs. His muscular arms constricted around her. He pulled her back into the room.

They landed on the floor. Tears welled up in her eyes, she wept. He held her still. While soothing her, he reached for his phone and called her father.

Mr. Danishe heard a loud raucous from beneath his second-floor window. His phone rang at the same time. He debated which one needed urgent attention. Dashing out of bed, he glanced through the window. It shocked him to see his oldest son, Kayah, punching his driver with a firm fist. The younger brother, Onah, was bouncing around, punching the air with his fists. Mr. Danishe didn't bother to put on a shirt. He sprinted out of the room.

"Take me to the place where they cut Malina." Kayah grabbed the driver by his shirt, pulling him up so fast that the man's feet left the ground.

Clearly terrified, the driver babbled, "I ...sir..."

Kayah threw the man down. He shoved another punch in his face. "Where is it?"

"Stop! Kayah," his father roared. "What is going on?"

"I want to know where they cut Malina. I'll burn it down," Kayah retorted. "After I burn it, I'll get the police to arrest all the idiots who did it to her."

"Kayah!" Mr. Danishe called in a worried tone. "Come inside." Kayah remained agitated, flexing his muscles furiously. "Please, son. Come inside."

Kayah pulled up the sleeves of his shirt, meanly eyeing the driver. The stepmother walked into the scene. He turned on her, "You made them cut her, even when she told you she didn't want it."

"It's our tradition," the stepmother replied mildly.

"Do you force a tradition on someone?" Kayah asked roughly. "You want to see her suffer. She could be dead right now. Are you happy?"

Mr. Danishe pushed his wife back, silencing her with his eyes. He dismissed several members of his household staff who have now gathered to watch the drama. "Who called you? Get back to work," he yelled at them. He beckoned Kayah to follow him inside the house. Kayah obliged him, followed by Onah.

Mr. Danishe spoke as soon as they entered the living room. "We haven't seen Malina since yesterday. I'm sure she's safe somewhere. I have sent my men out to look for her."

"Malina better be alive," Kayah grounded out. "Or someone will die."

"Calm down, son," Mr. Danishe muttered.

"Dad, I told you how I felt about this matter after I returned from Somalia. Why would you allow them to do it?"

Mr. Danishe made eye contact with his wife before saying, "It's what we've done for centuries. I can't let my daughter be different."

"I'll never forgive you, dad. If mom were alive, she'd have protected Malina."

"Yes, she would have," Onah concurred.

"Be quiet!" Mr. Danishe shut him up.

Ignoring the command, Onah continued. "I have seen with my own eyes what they do to girls."

"Onah!" Mr. Danishe cautioned him.

"Let him speak, dad. Please," Kayah pleaded.

Onah felt empowered to speak. "When I was in junior secondary school, I often took a shortcut, going behind people's yard to get to school. Many times, I would hear girls crying in papa Hinha compound. I wondered why? It wasn't a health center or maternity. One day, hiding in the bush, I saw two women bring a girl to the house. I could see their figures through the bamboo fence. I poked a hole through bamboo and saw the girl on the floor, naked. The two women held the girl's legs open. Hinha's grandmother used one hand to pull up something from between her legs and used a razor to cut it." He demonstrated it with his hands. "Blood splashed everywhere. The scream from her mouth sent me running. It scared me. Shaking like a leaf, I ran as if an evil masquerade was chasing me. I later found out they did circumcision on her."

"Curiosity killed the cat." The stepmother rebuked him. "Foolish boy. Who sent you?"

"Till today, what I saw that day still troubles me." Shuddering, Onah added. "Malina too..."

"Enough!" Mr. Danishe yelled.

"Dad, as a reporter, I have travelled the world and covered many subjects," Kayah spoke densely. All eyes turned to him. "I think it's time you see us as men, not boys. Remember Maya, the girl you wanted me to marry. Do you know why it didn't happen?" His father shook his head. "Every time I tried to make love to her, the condom broke. Even the lubricated ones. Let me give you this example. When you drive on an untarred road, your tires bounce up and down, making you tense and upset, but when you drive on a newly tarred road, your tires roll smoothly, you relax and enjoy the ride. The cut off thing that Onah saw is what makes sex enjoyable. Sleeping with Maya was like when rubber meets a dry road during harmattan and the rubber breaks. I tried other ways. She didn't enjoy what I was doing. It was like I bothered her with all my attempts. I got frustrated and ended the relationship."

Looking confused, the stepmother asked, "Was she supposed to enjoy it?"

"Yes, mother. It's for two people, not one." Kayah turned to his father. "Dad, you want Malina to marry, but you may send her to a very miserable life when her husband finds her stiff on his bed."

There was a deep silence in the room. The stepmother's phone rang. She answered the phone, and her face lit up. "It's Ayoni. Malina is with him."

"Thank God!" Kayah jumped to his feet. "Let's go get her," he said to Onah. The two rushed out of the house.

Chapter 8

Lagos Local Airport, Nigeria

Babza sat, flipping through a newspaper. He heard someone call, "Babu!" His heart skipped a beat. The voice from his vision has found him. He turned his head from side to side, trying to confirm his suspicion. He exhaled when he saw Candice, walking towards him.

"You look like you saw a ghost," Candice said as soon as she was within his earshot. "Are you okay?"

"Sure, I'm okay," he lied. "So good to see you." They attempted to hug but stopped. "This is COVID time," he said. They laughed. "What are you doing here?" He leaned back, looking her all over. "You look good."

"Thank you. I just flew in. Heading home to see my father. His birthday is coming up this weekend."

"I'm going home too. Now that I think of it, my dad's birthday is this weekend. What a coincidence." He looked at his watch. "Departure won't be for another hour. I came early to beat the traffic."

Candice knew from experience that what may look like a coincidence often turns out a prearranged crossing by fate. "Let's sit in the lounge," she suggested, already in motion.

They took two seats.

Babza rested his briefcase on the table. "Compared to the last time I saw you, you look incredibly relaxed," he complimented her again.

"I've lived with less stress since I left here," Candice returned lightly

"Yes, you put up a good fight to save that girl."

"Her name is Bekyah. And thanks for your help. We all did it."

He turned his face down, debating if he should share his new dilemma.

Candice was quick to see the change in his countenance. "Is something bothering you?"

He might as well share it. "Yes. What I'm about to tell you is strange. I'm still processing it."

"Okay." Candice nudged him to continue.

"It happened in my office," he began. After narrating the vision, he said, "I don't know what to make of it."

"You said you wrote it down." He nodded. "Let me see it."

He handed her a paper with his written notes. She read through and then gazed at a distance, thinking. "These are all scenes from the bible."

"Yes."

"Have you had something similar before?"

"No."

"Tell me what preceded the vision. What were you doing?"

He told her about the conversation with Kayah, the missing sister, and her circumcision.

An awakening came upon Candice. The dream that she had pushed aside as unimportant came fully alive in her mind. Her palms curved to cover her mouth. She gawked at Babza. "You're the one," she muffled beneath her palms.

"What did you say?"

An announcement for departure came through the PA system. Candice had no time to answer him. "I'll tell you later."

They joined the queue with other passengers who were rushing to get to the plane.

Candice emerged from the arrival hall to find her cousins waiting to take her home. She signaled to Babza to join her.

Approaching her, he said, "My brother is here to get me. I thought I could talk to you onboard, but the plane was full."

"That's okay. We're both here. We'll catch up."

"I will be at your house first thing tomorrow morning."

"Sounds good. See you then." She left with her cousins.

Ologne Village, Nigeria

Joyful cheers and jubilation met Candice at the entrance of her father's compound. Behind the fenced wall, men beat on drums and gongs. Women and girls danced to the music, they gyrated towards her. She threw down her carryon luggage, raised her hands and danced to meet with them.

Spreading her hands, Anowle, her aunt, jumped ahead of the group to come before Candice. "Amah is here! Daughter of our land, the Atewah of Ologne, welcome home."

"Thank you, aunty." Candice lightly embraced her. She turned to see her father standing by the door of his house. She hastened to meet with him. "Papa, I'm so glad to see you."

"Welcome home, Amah." He walked her inside the house. "Now I can rest."

"Do you still have malaria?"

"No. I'm much, much better now that I see you."

"That was a pleasant welcome." She pointed to the gathering outside the door.

"You are worth a lot to us. They were happy to wait for you."

"Thank you, papa."

They engaged in a chit-chat about the current events in the village.

Chapter 9

Babza's brother, Farakhi and their father, Chief Tabor, listened attentively to Babza as he narrated his vision. When he finished, he turned to his father, "Papa, you're a leader in your church. What do you make of it?"

"All the things you have said are in the bible. I don't know why you dreamt about them," Chief Tabor replied. "Did you attend a Bible class?"

"No." Babza's face creased. "I don't even own a bible."

"I suggest you take him to the pastor," Farakhi said to their father.

"That's a good idea," Chief Tabor concurred. "I will call him now." He briskly walked to his desk and called the pastor. "He can see us this afternoon."

"Okay." Babza stood up. "I'll go see Candice this morning."

"Amah is she in town?" Chief Tabor asked.

"Yes. We met at the airport in Lagos. We flew in together. I told her."

"What did she say?" Farakhi asked.

"We didn't get to talk about it. That's why I'm going to see her."

"Greet her father," Chief Tabor said.

A male servant was at the gate to welcome Babza to the Osunih's house. The servant walked him to a smaller house behind the main house. In the living room, sitting behind a desk, Candice hunched over a book. She looked up to see Babza enter the room.

"Good morning." She smiled, receiving him cheerfully.

"Good morning. Hope I didn't get you up early just to see me."

"No. I went to morning mass with my father already." She invited him to sit at the table with her. "I was reading this." She pointed a finger to a book, the Holy Bible. "I'm researching some things you told me yesterday."

"You're amazing. I didn't think to do that."

She laughed. "Reading the bible is a way of life. If you don't use it in your normal routine, you certainly won't use it when faced with the mysterious. Look at this book." She lifted a huge King James Version of the bible. "It's an enormous book. Where would you start?" Laying the book on the table, she added, "This is my father's bible. I'm not familiar with it. The American Bible Society version is preferable, the language is easier to read. I'm reading this slowly like a six-year-old child."

"Now, I don't feel so bad."

She stood up. "Let me get some paper and pen. I have to write some things down." Stopping at the door, she turned to him. "You want tea or coffee?"

"Coffee."

She came back a few minutes later with two pens and several sheets of letter-size blank papers. Behind her was a servant, holding a tray that contained two cups, a flask, sugar, and milk. He served the coffee and left.

Candice grabbed some sheets of paper and pen. She handed them to Babza. She did the same for herself.

"If you don't mind, please tell me the vision again."

"Here, I wrote it down." He reached into his pocket.

Candice stopped him. "I'm a visual person. Let me follow you with my mind's eyes to see what you saw. I couldn't do that at the airport. Too much noise from planes landing and taking off."

"Okay." Babza closed his eyes momentarily. Candice took deep breaths, opening her ears, heart, and mind to follow him.

He recounted his vision.

Candice wrote as he spoke. She gazed at her notes when he ended. "I wrote some points that stood out. You saw a place with angels, the garden of Eden, Adam and Eve and the serpent, Abraham in conversation with God, Sarah, whose 7 husbands died until she married Tobias, and lastly the dragon and the pregnant woman."

"Right. That sums it up." Babza nodded in agreement.

Touching the bible, Candice said, "Most of your vision are things that happened in the Old Testament. The last piece is in the last book of the New Testament."

"What does that mean?"

"I don't know." They were silent, thinking. Candice remembered something. "This morning, walking back home from church, my father stopped to buy a newspaper. I kept walking, but slowly so he could catch up with me. I heard a quiet voice whisper in my ear, 'the interrogation'. I looked around but saw no one close by. I shook it off. I wonder if the two words have anything to do with your vision." No answer or thoughts came from Babza. "At the airport, you said what preceded the vision was your friend who contacted you about his sister."

"Yes. They circumcised her against her wish. She ran away from home."

This is an 'aha' moment, Candice thought. "I get it. This is about female circumcision. I told you I had a dream in America."

"Yes. Sorry, I've been so preoccupied with my thoughts. I forgot to ask you about it."

"The tall guy in my dream told me saving Bekyah was the prelude for the actual job."

Babza shook his head to show a lack of understanding. "I run an advertising company, not a bible or philosophy school. Speak to me in plain language."

"The only thing I can tell you right now is we're involved in this because of female circumcision. I have no clue to what the job is and how your vision relates."

Babza glanced at his wristwatch. "I'm meeting with my father. We have an appointment with his pastor at the evangelical church." He stood up, heading towards the door.

Candice jumped to her feet. "Is it okay if I come along?"

"Why not. Please come."

They headed out.

Chapter 10

Babza and Candice arrived at Pastor Odio's house to meet Chief Tabor already seated in the pastor's living room. After the exchange of greetings, the pastor invited them to sit on a two-seater couch. To Babza, Pastor Odio said, "Your father has briefed me on what you told him. But before we talk, let us pray." They all stood up. "Almighty God, the El Sheda! The great 'I am'. You're the creator of the universe and everything in it. We praise you! Al maka sh…" he spoke in tongues. He concluded by saying, "In the mighty name of Jesus."

"Amen!"

"Please sit down," Pastor Odio told them. He addressed Babza, "Chief said you have everything written. Can I see the paper?" Babza produced it from his pocket and gave it to him. He studied it for a little while, then got up to bring his bible. "What you saw goes from the book of Genesis to Revelation. There's not much said in between to give us what they all mean."

Candice interjected, "I've gathered that female circumcision may be the focus."

"Eh, we don't do that anymore," Pastor Odio remarked.

44

"We are one community," Candice returned. "They practice it in several communities in Nigeria and about 30 countries around the world, many in Africa, Middle East, and as far as Asia."

"Ah!" Pastor Odio exclaimed. "I didn't know it's that widespread."

"Pastor," Chief Tabor called his attention. "What do you say my son should do?"

The pastor gazed intently at Babza's sheet in his hand. "I don't remember this Tobias and Sarah."

"It's in the Douia Catholic Bible," Candice pointed out.

"Oh, okay. I will pray and fast over this. Give me till tomorrow."

Believing that they were dismissed, Babza stood up. "Thank you for seeing us. We will talk again tomorrow."

Outside the pastor's house, Candice and Babza parted ways with Chief Tabor. On the drive to Candice's house, she saw her father.

"Babza, pulled the car over, let me talk to my father."

He pulled the car by the curb.

Candice got out of the car. She walked to meet with her father. "Papa, are you going to the parish?"

"Yes. I have a meeting with the priest. I was told you left home."

"Yes. Sorry, I didn't tell you. I had to follow Babza to see Pastor Odio."

"I hope everything is okay."

"Hmm," she moaned. "Do you think the priest will have a minute to see us?"

"I don't know. Let's go to the parish and find out."

"Alright. I'll walk with you so I can brief you on what's going on. Let me tell Babza to go to the parish, ahead of us." She informed him of the change in plans. On the walk with her father, she shared Babza's vision.

"This is very interesting," the Osunih said when she concluded. "Let's see what Father Jacobs would say."

Reverend Father Jacobs sat with Babza, Candice, and the Osunih when his meeting ended. Babza told his vision, speaking slowly for clarity. Within him, he felt more at ease the more he recounted it. He remembered more details with each repetition. From what Candice pointed out to him, the events in the vision had a beginning and an end. Bible stories weren't familiar to him, but he was a perceptive entrepreneur. He'd begin with the end, using it as a guide. He addressed the priest. "Father, the last thing he told me was the woman and the dragon. Could you explain it to me?"

"That's in the book of Revelation 12. The short version is the woman in the book represents Israel. She had a crown on her head with 12 stars which represent the 12 tribes of Israel. Israel will give birth to a male child who will rule the world. The child is the messiah. The dragon is Satan, who rebelled against God. Satan wanted to destroy Israel and her child, Jesus. There was a fight in heaven, Satan was defeated and thrown down to earth with a third of heavenly angels who supported him."

Candice made a note for herself. "What are the 12 tribes of Israel?"

"They are Reuben, Simeon, Judah, Issachar, Zebulun, Benjamin, Dan, Naphtali, Gad, Asher, Ephraim, and Manasseh."

Nothing important jumped at her. She went up the ladder. The woman whose 7 husbands died came next. "Father, what killed Sarah's 7 husbands before Tobias?"

"I asked that same question. The Voice didn't give me an answer," Babza uttered.

"A devil killed them on their wedding night. Tobias escaped death through fasting and prayers."

"Okay, let's move up the ladder," Candice said. "The next one is Abraham and the covenant with God. The males were to circumcise, not female."

"That's correct," Father Jacobs replied.

"I'm trying to find the common denominator in all the scenes. Women were involved in the other two. Even though you said the woman with the sun represents Israel, as a layperson, I will leave her as a woman for now." She stayed pensive for a minute. "There was no woman at all in the scene with Abraham and God."

"Let's move to the next one." Babza nudged her to continue.

"The last scene up the ladder is the creation of Adam and Eve. And how the serpent tricked her into eating the forbidden apple."

"The serpent was Satan," Father Jacobs clarified.

"In three of the four scenes, there was Satan and a woman. And in all three, Satan intended to hurt the woman directly or indirectly. Am I correct?" Candice asked.

"Yes." The men responded simultaneously.

"Looks like Satan is antagonistic towards these women," Babza surmised.

"The question is why? And why was the scene with Abraham included in your vision?" Candice directed her eyes at Babza.

"I don't know." He looked genially sincere.

She looked at the other two. They shook their heads. She searched her brain for answers; she came up with a blank. "I want to suggest we stop today and continue our discussion tomorrow. Something may click overnight."

"Sounds good," Babza agreed. He stood up. The others followed. They languidly walked to the door.

At the door, Father Jacobs said, "I will read the book of Genesis tonight and meditate on it." They lingered by the door. "In Genesis, you find what St. Augustine called the interrogation of temptations."

Candice's felt her heartbeat race. "Did you say the interrogation?" The priest gazed at her. "This morning, on my way from church, I heard a voice in my head say, 'the interrogation.' I didn't know what to make of it."

Babza acknowledge her statement. "You mentioned it this morning."

"I want to hear about it," Candice shifted closer to the door.

"Not now." Babza pulled her back. "We will continue tomorrow. We need to eat."

Candice reluctantly agreed. "Tomorrow, then."

They parted ways.

Chapter 11

Candice engaged in a monologue by her grandmother's grave, located deep in the yard behind their house. Even though she didn't expect any kind of dialogue from her grandmother, voicing her thoughts brought her comfort. Were her grandmother alive, she would have imparted words of wisdom to her. In her mind, she wrestled with the current situation at hand. Recapping from yesterday, there was a conflict between Satan and the women, enough to cause enmity between them. 'Enmity.' The word sounded familiar. Where has she heard it? She lowered her head to recollect. God said it to the serpent after Adam and Eve ate the forbidden apple. Hum, that scene was part of Babza's vision. She'd read the bible verse for an understanding. That resolved, a warmth within propelled her to move. She turned to leave and ran into her father.

"Papa, good morning."

"Good morning, my daughter. I thought I'll find you here."

"Visiting grandmother always comforts me."
She turned half-circle with her eyes sweeping the area.

"Hmm," he groaned. He pointed to the garden close by the grave. "That was her favorite place. She spent a lot of time in this area."

"She came here a lot?"

"Yes, she was at home here." He looked tenderly at Candice. "I'm glad you still find time to connect with your grandmother."

"Uh hum," Candice murmured.

"There's a car waiting for you outside. Babza sent a driver to bring you to their house."

"I'm done here." She walked towards the house. She halted, turning to him. "Papa, come too. I spoke to Father Jacobs this morning. I invited him for a continuation of our discussion at Chief Tabor's house."

"Okay. I will come."

In Chief Tabor's living room sat Babza, Farakhi, Chief Tabor, and Pastor Odio. A servant announced Candice and the Osunih. Babza welcomed them. Shortly after, the servant announced Father Jacobs. Several maidservants brought in refreshments and served the guests.

Chief Tabor welcomed everyone and thanked them for joining efforts to help his son. He turned to Pastor Odio. "Pastor, please tell us what you told me on the phone this morning."

"Good morning, everyone. God be with you all." The pastor waited for their responses. "I sought the Lord on this matter. The spirit kept showing me, Father Abraham. Why Abraham? I asked. I read the holy book about him all night."

Babza's brow arched. "It was his covenant with God that was brought to my attention."

"I know, but sometimes you have to read the complete text to make sense of it all." When no one spoke, he continued. "I will give you a short version of Abraham's life before the one in Babza's vision. In Genesis 12: 10-20, Abraham was called Abram before God changed it to Abraham. He was married to Sarai. There was a famine in the land where Abram settled. He went to Egypt to live as an immigrant. On their way to Egypt, Abram asked his wife to pretend to be his sister because he was afraid that they may kill him and take her because she was very beautiful. He reasoned that if they knew she was his sister, not his wife, they will treat him well for her sake, and he will survive. In Egypt, Pharaoh was interested in her. Things went well for Abram for a while. He gained wealth, flocks, cattle, donkeys, camels, plus male and female servants.

Then the Lord struck Pharaoh and his household with severe plague for taking Abram's wife. Pharaoh found out about Abram's deceit and sent him, his wife, his nephew, Lot, and everything he owed out of Egypt. Pharaoh gave Abram plenty of presents as gifts of forgiveness and repentance.

In the land that Abram and Lot settled, conflicts broke out between Abram and Lot's herdsmen, so they separated, each to a different land. There were wars here and there. The Lord settled Abram in the land from Egypt's river to the areas around the great Euphrates.

Abram's wife couldn't have children. On the wife's instruction, their Egyptian servant Hagar had a son, Ishmael, for Abram. At age 99, the Lord God appeared to Abram. God changed his name to Abraham. God told Abraham that he will be a father of many descendants and

51

nations for many generations. His descendants will produce many kings. God made a covenant with Abraham; he must circumcise every male in his household, including the servants and the slaves he bought from foreigners. They must circumcise all male children on the eight-day after birth. God said he will cut from his people any male whose flesh of his foreskin is uncircumcised. They will not be his people. God changed the wife's name from Sarai to Sarah. At age 90, she had a son, Isaac. Many generations later, Jesus came as a descendant of Abraham."

"Very informative," Babza uttered after the pastor finished.

"I'm still trying to find the common denominator here," Candice spoke aloud. "Her husband used the woman, Sarai, to favor himself."

"They found out," Farakhi said. "And they threw them out."

"With lots of wealth," Babza added.

"Not bad," Candice rejoined. She turned to Father Jacobs. "You mentioned the interrogation yesterday."

"Yes," Father Jacobs responded. "God wants to bring humanity to Himself. To live a faithful life and bring himself to God, man must submit to trials to know his strength through his actions. To do or not to do? This often poses a challenge. To find himself, man must confront his fears in what St. Augustine called, 'The Interrogation of Temptation.' Every decision should be measured against the Word of God. We are on the right path when the action taken during the interrogation aligns with God's desires. St. Augustine said our actions should be underlined with love, not with inflated pride. A fully developed spirit rejoices when the prideful ego is disappointed; it means that man has discovered the meaning of true love. This is what Satan does not want."

Candice sought more clarification. "You mean Satan uses our ego or pride to push us to act against God's command?"

"Yes. Pride and other strategies. The interrogation has been with us since the serpent visited the woman in the garden of Eden. In Genesis 3, the serpent asked Eve, 'Did God really tell you not to eat fruit from the tree of knowledge of good and evil?' Satan initiated a sense of doubt and confusion in her, making her doubt if she heard the command correctly. Then Satan promoted speculation; if fear for her safety had been a deterrent for disobedience, Satan assured her not to worry. There was no consequence if she disobeyed God. He told her, 'You surely will not die.' Satan then hit her with the ultimate assault on the senses. He told her, 'You will be like God,' a pride-filled ambition. She caved in. The scrutiny has continued to plague humanity as Satan plays trickery on our senses. He constantly challenges us to take the bait."

"You're correct," Pastor Odio responded. "In Ephesian 6:12, Paul tells us that we do not wrestle against flesh and blood, but against principalities, powers, and the rulers of the darkness of this world and against spiritual hosts of wickedness in heavenly places."

"Mind you," Father Jacobs continued. "In the desert, after Jesus fasted for forty days, Satan used the same tactics to tempt Jesus."

"Yes," concurred Pastor Odio. "Those two scenes are the two documented direct tactics used by Satan."

"Eve fell for it, but Jesus didn't," Chief Tabor uttered.

"Yes," Father Jacobs responded.

"I now know how the interrogation plays out." Candice looked at both men of God. "I have another word I'm trying to figure out, enmity. I know God used it. Can you both shed more light on it?"

Both men looked at each other, accessing who should go first.

Pastor Odio took the lead. "After Satan made Eve eat the forbidden fruit, she gave the fruit to Adam, and he ate it. All three received consequences for their actions. God told the serpent, 'Because you have done this, you are cursed more than every beast of the field, on your belly, you shall crawl, and you shall eat dust all the days of your life'. And God added, 'I will put enmity between you and the woman, between your seed and her seed; he shall crush your head, and you shall bruise his heel'. God told the woman, 'I will increase your pains in childbearing, your desire shall be for your husband, and he shall rule over you.' God told Adam, 'Cursed is the ground for your sake, in toil you shall eat of it, all the days of your life.'"

Father Jacobs exhaled. "I want to point out here, the serpent was the only one that got cursed directly. The curse was an invocation of harm or destruction on it. God diverged the curse on Adam to the ground, which means he will now exert more energy to find food. Eve did not receive an invocation of harm either; she got a decree that reprimanded her disobedience. More pain in childbirth and she would only desire her husband, not seek egoist ambition."

Babza thought he has had enough. "I still don't see how they all tie up to my vision."

"This is plenty of bible lessons for me," Farakhi stated.

"Maybe we should let all we've heard sink in," the Osunih said.

"I agree. Let's continue tomorrow," Chief Tabor voiced.

Candice pressed her lips together, with her eyes narrowing. "All these discussions have expanded Babza's vision, linking them to events in the Bible. I still don't see the common denominator." She briefly lowered her head into her palms. She raised her head, looking directly at Babza. "In my dream, I was told you would uncover the truth. My question for you is, what are we trying to uncover? Maybe if we know what we are looking for, everything will make sense."

Babza exhaled. "I honestly don't know."

Candice smoothed her hair back. "Let me try again? What were you thinking before the vision?"

Babza tried to recall. "It was about my friend's sister who ran away from home after being circumcised."

"That was an event that happened." She pressed further, "It must have roused something inside you, something that needed an explanation or a question."

"I don't remember any question." A little irked with the probing, Babza's face wrinkled.

"Please," Candice said gently. She gently held his hand. "Go back to that day. Try to remember what was on your mind before you fell asleep. It might give us a clue."

Babza leaned back on his chair and lifted his face to the ceiling. Candice shifted close to him and knelt in front of him. She rested her hands on both his knees.

Babza felt the warmth of her touch. It radiated through his body. Relaxing, he drifted back to that day. He remembered feeling the beginning of a headache. Before that, he had wondered how long will this continue to plague his world, and who started it? He suddenly looked down to face Candice. "I remember thinking about my experience with a woman I had dated. The relationship broke up because of her circumcision. It troubled me. I wondered how long would I keep hearing about this? Then I said to myself, 'who the hell started it?'" His eyes lit up. "That's it! I wanted to know who started it?"

Candice jumped to her feet. "Thank God. We have the question and the goal. The answer is somewhere in the vision."

"That explains the tour," Babza responded.

"Since we're looking for a 'who' we can now find ..."

"The common denominator," Farakhi concluded for her, laughing.

"And possibly the motive," Babza added.

"Good," Chief Tabor commented. "We will continue tomorrow. They have prepared lunch. Let's eat."

Chapter 12

Candice felt the warmth of the morning sun on her face, she lifted her head to breath in the crisp air. Babza walked into the courtyard to join her.

"Thanks for coming early." His tone was filled with gratitude.

"I couldn't sleep, anyway," Candice returned.

"Me, too. There's too much stuff to take in."

"I'm glad that we have a goal now."

"Amah..."

Candice cut him off. "I get suspicious when you call me Amah." She spoke with amusement in her voice.

He laughed. "Yesterday, you pushed me till I got to the core of myself. The goal was buried in there. Calling you Amah is too simple. It should be Princess Amah."

"I thought I was the Atewah of Ologne."

"Atewah, you are. It's an inherited title of honor. If you lived in this community, you would receive the same royal treatment as those who live in the king's palace. That makes you a princess."

"Okay. Prince Babza." She genuflected lightly before him. "I accept."

"Glad we settled that." Babza smiled. They walked further into the courtyard. "I appreciate your presence. Thank you."

"My pleasure. Back to the business at hand. My father and the priest should join us soon."

"I put on my business hat late last night. I sorted and plugged the information we gathered into a chart. The posterboard is in the living room."

The gate slowly opened. Pastor Odio's car entered the compound. He emerged from the car. Babza and Candice met with him. They exchanged greetings and entered the house.

Farakhi sat on a chair, and in a conversation with Chief Tabor.

Minutes later, the Osunih and Father Jacobs joined the group.

Farakhi stood up. "You are all welcome to my father's house. Please sit down."

"Thank you." The guests responded, taking their seats.

Farakhi returned to his seat.

Babza presented his posterboard. "I have plugged the events and the major characters in our discussions on this chart. I broke them into groups.

Group 1: The angels, Lucifer/Satan, Adam, and Eve. Inscribed beside them are the temptation, the curse, and the decree.

Group 2: Abraham and Sarah. Inscribed beside them are migration, lies, father of many nations and the covenant of circumcision.

Group 3: Tobias and Sarah. Inscribed beside them are the Devil/Satan and the 7 dead husbands.

Group 4: A pregnant woman with the Sun, and the Dragon/Satan. We're also told that a fight broke out in heaven and the Dragon/Satan and his supports were thrown down to earth.

Group 5: Malina, she represents all females who have been subjected to circumcision.

At the bottom of the chart is a question. Who started female circumcision and what is the motive?"

Babza scanned everyone's face. They looked puzzled, but attentive. "I used Candice's approach. Satan appeared in groups 1, 3, and 4. Men appeared in groups 1,2, and 3. Women appeared in all five groups."

"I don't think we should count the dead husbands," Farakhi said.

Pastor Odio leaned forward, studying the chart. "Circumcision appears in groups 2 and 5 where Satan is not mentioned."

"I can bet that Satan is connected to those two groups," Candice voiced her thoughts with deep conviction.

Babza stood up, lifted his right hand, and signaled Candice to follow him. To the others, he said, "Please excuse us for a minute." He walked with Candice to the kitchen. He turned Candice to face him. "At the beginning of my vision, angels were rejoicing except one, Satan. He was pouting, looking at the humans with disgust." He hesitated, thinking.

"Go on, what else?"

"The Voice told me Satan took the form of a snake, came to hang on the tree to get the woman's attention even before it spoke to her. It later convinced her to eat the forbidden fruit." Babza's eyes narrowed reflectively. "Satan deliberately went after Eve."

"You're very perceptive, Babu," Candice uttered.

Her words rang a bell in his head. He heard that before, from the Voice right after he said the snake was a clever interloper. He shared his thoughts with Candice.

"I knew it! Satan is after women. We have to find out why?" She suddenly searched herself. "I don't have my phone on me. Do you have yours?" Babza withdrew his phone from his pocket. "Unlock it, please."

"What are you doing?"

"I want to google the meaning of interloper." She searched and read aloud. "A person who becomes involved in a place or situation where they are not wanted or belong." She kept searching. "Other similar words are meddler, intruder, thief, burglar, alien."

"Interesting," Babza uttered. "I was told Lucifer was a high angel and very smart. God gave him power and position in a high place."

"I've also heard that Satan is a usurper. He wants to usurp God's throne and take over creation," Candice stated.

"Meaning he has the power to meddle in any situation to his advantage," Babza added.

"Yes. Mostly to bring confusion."

"And he began with Eve." Babza nodded his head, convincingly. "I propose a hypothesis, Satan introduced female circumcision."

"To discredit God?"

"Yes. My questions are why use the woman's genitals to achieve his ambitious rebellion against God and how did he do it?"

"I don't know. We have to dig some more."

He nudged her to follow him. "Let's get back to the group."

Babza and Candice explained their discussion to the group, the hypotheses, and the questions.

Babza pulled a chair from the dining room to the living room. He displayed the posterboard on the chair. He turned to the men of God. "We learned that Satan tempted Eve. Why was he in the garden to tempt her?"

Father Jacobs cleared his throat. "Let's begin with what happened before the creation of Adam and Eve. In a heavenly place, lived the Tri-union God and the angels. The angels had free will. They worshipped God, protected God's kingdom and God's throne. They had a hierarchy of positions and functions. Among the high angels was Lucifer, meaning the light-bearer. In Ezekiel 28:12-17, we find a gathered description of Lucifer. He was a highly dignified angel, very majestic in appearance, and intellectually astute. God granted him power and position. He shone in splendor. He became very prideful and wanted to be glorified with God. The name Lucifer changed to Satan because of his evil ways. He rebelled against God, and they pushed him out of heaven."

"Yes," Pastor Odio joined in. "Even though they kicked him out of heaven, he could still go between heaven and earth."

"What do you mean?" Farakhi asked.

"In the book of Job 1:6-7," Pastor Odio clarified. "God asked Satan where he came from? Satan answered, he came from roaming about on the earth."

Father Jacobs took over, "On earth, God first created man, Adam, and then created the woman, Eve. They were created in his image. They would multiply and fill the earth. Even though humans were created lower than the angels, they were crowned with glory and honor and given dominion over all that God has created on earth. God's design for humanity was through grace they will be with him in heaven when their time on earth was over. God put Adam and Eve in the garden of Eden. They were free to eat all fruits except from one tree that gives the knowledge of good and evil. God gave them free will.

For Satan, the thought that God designed humankind to be with him in heaven, a place where they kicked him out, must have infuriated him. Like a jealous ex-boyfriend who tells his ex-girlfriend that since you don't want me, you can't have others, Satan set up a strategy to disrupt God's plan. He knew if man disobeyed God, they would never return to God. They would be under his influence forever. Satan entered the garden to corrupt Adam and Eve."

Pastor Odio interjected, "From Ezekiel 28:13, we inferred that Satan lived in the garden of Eden before he turned evil. So, he was familiar with the environment."

"Eh!" The Osunih shook his head lightly. "This is why our people say, keep an eye on your wayward child that you kicked out of your house, they will come back to haunt you."

"And corrupt the rest of your children," Chief Tabor added.

Father Jacobs resumed, "Satan tempted Eve first. I think because she was the most vulnerable, the newest kid on the block. The bible tells us God put Adam to sleep, and then took his rib to create Eve. Adam was asleep, I'm sure Satan wasn't. He watched God meticulously and delicately put all her body parts together, including the fine details. She was God's last created creature and the vessel that will bring forth more humans. Eve and her womb would be of interest to Satan. He didn't want the multiplication of humans so that less would end up in heaven to be with God. Eve was a good place to begin his rivalry against God. He manipulated God's instruction and she fell for his tricks. He knew Adam would fall too. Both were banished from the garden."

Babza summed his understanding of Satan's presence in the garden. "Satan despised the eventual unification of humanity with God. His scheme displaced Adam and Eve from the garden, aiming to keep them under his leadership."

"To cause division between humans and God," Father Jacobs repeated firmly. "He will then destroy humanity."

"He succeeded," Farakhi commented.

"Yes, the disobedience of Adam and Eve caused a spiritual separation between the humans and God," Father Jacobs emphasized. "God put a curse on Satan for tricking Adam and Eve and added that the woman's seed would crush his head. He now faced another problem, the fear of being crushed by the woman's seed. Like an angry lion, his fury escalated."

Pastor Odio interjected, "It is written in 1 Peter 5:8, 'your enemy, the devil lurks around like a roaring lion looking for someone to devour.' To support what brother Jacobs said about Satan hating people, Cain killed Abel; one line of descendants went down. God had to put a mark on Cain so that no one would hurt him. Otherwise,

Satan would go after Cain. Humans started multiplying, Satan corrupted them. As narrated in Genesis 6: 5-8, God saw the wickedness of humans, and he wiped them all out with a flood. Only Noah and his family, and some numbered living things, were saved. God had to start afresh. We see again in Genesis 13: 13, The Lord sent angels to destroy the people of Sodom and Gomorrah for their wickedness and sin against God. In short, Satan's reason for existence is to prevent humans from uniting with God either by ruling and/or killing them."

Turning to both men of God, Farakhi said, "Thank you for that explanation, I have a better understanding."

"We have established that Satan had the motive and access to the woman," Babza stated. "We want to know why he chose the woman's genitals as a weapon."

"It is all because of sex," the Osunih answered. "We even heard that the apple they ate was sex that they did."

"Papa," Candice directed her attention to the Osunih. "The apple can't be sex. God created the woman for Adam to procreate. It was likely that they'd have sex to make children." Awakening suddenly dawned on her. "That's it! It's her ability to bear children."

"Why would he have a problem with that?" Chief Tabor asked.

"When God told the serpent that the woman's seed or offspring would crush its head, Satan knew that was meant for him," Pastor Odio responded. "He didn't want her to have children."

"I get it," Candice said elatedly. "To protect himself, he went after her."

"Yes," Father Jacobs concurred. "He went on the offense; destroy the woman and her progeny so that her seed would not crush him. And two, reduce the number of humans that would make it to heaven. Satan knew the incarnate God would come to set those under his influence free and lead them to God, but he didn't know when it would happen. Convinced that he'd tempt the incarnate God, too, he felt confident that he'd win the battle against God. He began his plot to accomplish his task."

"He wanted to destroy the very organ that would enable her to produce children," Candice concluded. She paused and gathered her composure. "He knew the effects of genital mutilation; she could die from excessive bleeding and infection. It could cause infertility, pain during intercourse, and it could make her undesirable to her husband. He could reject her when he finds out that they badly disfigured her genitals. Satan felt safe as long as no seed or children come out of her."

"Mutilating her was the best way to beat God. Hmm," Babza grunted. In his mind, he said, Satan hijacked her sexuality.

Babza thanked the men of God for enlightening them on Satan's motives. "This is the next question. How did Satan introduce the circumcision of females?"

"To answer that, I think we should look at the scene of Abraham and the covenant with God," Pastor Odio proposed. "That's the first place we heard of circumcision."

"I agree," Father Jacobs said. "Satan uses God's words to confuse people."

Pastor Odio continued, "God did two things with Abraham and his people. First, he granted them fertility. He promised Abraham that he will be the father of many nations, he'd have many descendants, some of them will be kings for many generations. What do you think went through Satan's head when God made this promise?"

"He must hate the idea of more humans," Father Jacobs responded. "And kings, for that matter, which means they will be powerful. We've been told Lucifer or Satan was a powerful angel. God promising power to some kings must be hard to bear. He was too conceited to share power with mere humans."

Pastor Odio rejoined. "After the flood, the curse that was put on the ground because of Adam's disobedience was lifted. Satan was the only one who still had a curse hanging over his head. Over time, as the population grew, so also grew the awareness that the woman's seed would one day come to destroy him. How would he protect himself?" It wasn't a question for them to answer. "God made a covenant of circumcision with Abraham. Bingo! Satan found the solution to his dilemma. He received the golden opportunity; he will use God's words to confuse the people. By mutilating her maybe the woman's seed will never be born. He was safe!"

"Hah!" Farakhi breathed out. "This is deep."

"We now have to find out how he used God's covenant to his advantage," Candice uttered.

Father Jacobs asserted, "Male circumcision symbolized a rebirth, removing the sins of the past, both theirs and their ancestors. Not that the organ itself had sin, it was the behavior of the people that was sinful. Abraham was agreeing to be set free from sin and become faithful to God forever. And he proved it when he almost sacrificed his son, Isaac. I'm sure that Abraham and his descendants being faithful to God forever would be too much for Satan to accept. That must have bothered him."

Pastor Odio nodded. "Bothered, but not give up."

All were quiet for a full minute. Babza broke the silence. "In my notes, Satan directly manipulated two people, Eve and Jesus. Let's see his operational techniques. From there, we can deduce how he introduced female circumcision."

"My people," Chief Tabor interrupted them. "It will be a long afternoon. Let's eat."

They all shifted to the dining room.

Chapter 13

A flash of joy lit Candice's face. She moved the mobile phone to her other ear. "That's good news, Celia. I'm proud of you. Congratulations!"

Babza entered the courtyard. He saw Candice absorbed in a conversation with the other party on the phone. He waited a few feet away; he didn't want to disturb her. She was as dazzling as she was when they were teenagers. After years of not seeing her, he didn't prepare for the effects of her presence on him. The pull was as strong as it was back then. It seemed to take hold of him whenever he was near her. He was careful not to let it show, but in the last few hours, it felt like he was failing woefully.

She saw him from the corners of her eyes. He was staring at her. Assuming they were ready to regroup, she hurried to finish her call. She met him, expecting him to announce the resumption of the meeting. Instead, his eyes burrowed into hers. He said nothing. "Are we ready to go back in?" she asked him. He was silent. She prodded him with a lift of her brow. He stood muted. She didn't know what to make of his silence. She lifted her head, making sure their eyes have direct contact. She spoke softly, "I know I put a lot of pressure on you back there. I'm sorry, I get pushy when I tackle something difficult."

"I love you." He finally put his feeling in words. A warm wave seemed to sweep through him, sending relief through his entire body.

Taken aback, she didn't know how to respond or what to say. She turned her back on him, walking away.

He went after her, got hold of her arm, and pulled her back. "Sorry, I didn't mean to shock you."

She dislodged his hold on her arm. She turned her face up and squinted at the sun. "I love the heat. My daughter told me the weather in New York is cold."

Babza got the message, avoidance. He'd leave it alone for now. "That was your daughter on the phone?"

"Yes. She was promoted to a managerial position."

"Smart kid. I'm not surprised though. She's like her mother."

"Thanks."

"Did you enjoy your lunch?"

"Yes, especially since I didn't prepare it."

"Ah, you like to be served."

"Not that. My life in New York is always in a rush. A good meal needs time for preparation. I have limited time."

"Oh, I see."

They turned at the sound of the opening gate.

Brea, Candice's niece, came into the yard. Candice quickly walked to her. She took Brea's hand. "Let me introduce you to my beautiful niece," she said to Babza. She introduced both to each other. There was a prideful undertone in the way she spoke about Brea. "She's super smart, and a final year medical student at the university."

Brea was modest in her response. "Thanks, aunty. I'm just a regular student."

"I asked her to do research on female circumcision," Candice said to Babza.

"I brought them to you." Brea handed a folder to Candice. "I can wait to explain what I found."

Candice looked at Babza for approval.

He nodded his head. "We need all the information we can get." He motioned them to go into the house. At the door, he pulled Candice, whispering, "We'll continue with our conversation when this is over."

In the living room, Brea presented her research to the group. "According to UNICEF's global database, about 200 million girls and women alive have undergone female circumcision in 30 countries from Asia to the Middle East and Africa. They said about another 68 million girls are likely to be cut by 2030 because of population growth."

"Small girl," Chief Tabor called Brea. "There are old people here. Talk slow, slow."

"Yes, sir," Brea responded. She lowered her voice inflection, "There are four different ways they cut the girls and women, and the styles differ from place to place. Type I is called clitoridectomy, it is the total or partial removal of the clitoris. They practice it in many African countries, from Ethiopia, Eritrea, Kenya, Nigeria, Benin to Senegal, and in Pakistan and India. Type II is the removal of the clitoris plus a portion of or all the labia minora (excision). They do it in regions of West Africa, such as Sierra Leone, and Guinea. Type III is the removal of the clitoris, removal of all the labia minora with the labia majora sewn together, leaving a small opening for urination and menstrual flow. Eighty percent of Type III, the most severe type, is done in Somalia. The fourth type is a combination of different practices."

"Aba, father!" Pastor Odio exclaimed. "I don't like what I'm hearing."

The Osunih cleared his throat. "How is it that all these countries that are scattered all over the place are doing this thing? Do they eat okra soup and pounded yam in Asia as we do here?"

"Do they eat fufu with melon soup and drink palm wine as we do here?" Farakhi asked.

"Good questions," Candice responded firmly. "I have pondered these questions. How come people in this small village in West Africa and people in Pakistan and India do this practice. We have nothing in common."

Farakhi looked puzzled. "You mean the Indian people we see in Bollywood movies? We don't even look like them."

"Christians, Muslims, and those who worship other gods like the sun god do it," Candice added.

"I see," Chief Tabor uttered. "So, Christians, Muslims, and Shango worshippers have finally agreed on this one thing. Maybe we all came from the same place, after all."

Candice offered an explanation. "Remember when Abram left Egypt, he went with his family, and servants who were Egyptians. There may be other groups of different backgrounds among them. We don't know."

Babza addressed the pastor, "God told Abraham to circumcise all males in his family including the slaves born in his house and those he bought from foreigners, right?"

"Yes," Pastor Odio answered.

71

"If Abraham bought slaves, that means there were slave traders who were foreigners in their mix. These foreigners could have come from lands far and near. Slave trade used to be a booming business. Judging from the amount of wealth Abraham possessed, he must have bought many. The traders may have returned to their home base or markets under the influence of Satan." Babza turned to Brea. "Continue."

"Yes, sir," Brea replied. "To confirm what my aunty said, they said people who migrate to other countries carry this practice to their new homes in places like England, Germany, France, and America."

Brea ended her presentation. They thanked her. Farakhi called a maid to take her to the dining room for lunch.

Babza narrowed his gaze on the notepad in his hand. "We have seen that the practice is widespread, covering several geographic areas. Let's see how Satan convinced the people to do it. As I said before the break, we will look at his operational techniques." Addressing Pastor Odio. "Please share the serpent's encounter with Eve."

Pastor Odio recounted the incident. "The serpent asked Eve, 'Did God really say, you must not eat from any tree in the garden'?'"

"Strategy number 1," Babza announced, "The serpent made Eve doubt if she heard the correct instruction. This is to confuse her. He also stirred her need to eat the fruit." He signaled to Pastor Odio to continue.

"Eve said, 'We must not eat fruit from the tree that is in the middle of the garden, and we must not touch it, or we will die. The serpent told her, 'You will certainly not die'."

"Strategy number 2, The serpent assured her of her safety. Told her to eat it, there is no consequence for disobedience. If she ate the fruit, she'd feel good."

Pastor Odio added the last trick. "The serpent told her, 'For God knows that when you eat from it your eyes will be opened, and you will be like God, knowing good and evil.'"

"Strategy number 3, The serpent elevated her self-importance or pride by telling her she will be like God. He used their experiences and knowledge of God's goodness to entice Eve to want to gain the attributes of God."

When they finished with the temptation of Eve, Babza turned to Father Jacobs, "Please share Satan's encounter with Jesus."

"Knowing very well that Jesus was hungry," Father Jacobs uttered. "He said to Jesus, 'If you are the Son of God, turn these stones to bread.'"

"Strategy number 1, He wanted Jesus to doubt his identity by asking, 'if you're the son of God.' Satan also brought Jesus' need for food to his attention."

Father Jacobs continued, "Satan said, 'If you are the Son of God, throw yourself down. For it is written, he will command his angels concerning you, and they will lift you up in their hands so that you will not strike your foot against a stone.'"

"Strategy number 2, Satan assured Jesus of his safety by saying if Jesus threw himself down, angels will not let him fall."

Father Jacobs threw in the last temptation. "The devil took him to a very high mountain and showed him all the kingdoms of the world and their splendor. All this I will give you, he said, 'if you will bow down and worship me.'"

"Strategy number 3, Satan tried to elevate Jesus' pride by promising to give Jesus the world. He used their experiences of the things of the world to entice him."

Babza let everyone think about the strategies. "The key tools he used were doubt, safety, and pride." He saw Brea walk into the room straight to Candice. She leaned over and whispered something in Candice's ear. Candice turned to him; with her head craned sideways, she signaled to him to follow her. "Excuse us for a minute," he told the group as he followed Candice and Brea to the kitchen.

In a low tone, Brea addressed Candice and Babza. "I have more information to share, but I stopped because old people are present."

"What is it?" Candice asked.

"It's about the different outcomes between female and male circumcision."

Candice deferred to Babza to allow Brea to address the group.

"Everyone is an adult. Come share what you have." Babza led them back to the room. He informed the group, saying, "Brea has more information to share with us."

"Thank you, sir," Brea said respectfully. "There are different results in the male circumcision compared to female circumcision. In the uncircumcised male's penis at rest, the foreskin is in folds, and it covers most of the top of the man's penis. The foreskin needs special attention to keep it clean from dirt and sweat. In the aroused penis, the foreskin pulls back to expose all the head of the penis. The most sensitive part of the penis is on the head." She presented a drawn picture of the penis for illustration. She pointed to the mentioned area.

"The rim of the penis is called the corona of glands, and the undersurface side where the corona curves forward from either side, towards the tip of the pee-hole is the frenulum of the prepuce. The corona of glands and the frenulum of the prepuce are the most sensitive parts of a man's penis. Men get the most pleasure there. In the uncircumcised male, this area is buried under the folds of the foreskin when the man is resting. For the circumcised man, this area is exposed and ready for action at the slightest whim. Even the wind can stir a man into action. In short, male circumcision gives a man a low maintenance organ and a quick access to his pleasure points." She paused.

The men shifted in their seats, adjusting positions.

"The outcome of female circumcision is different for women," Brea continued. "The external part of the female genitals is called the vulva." She showed them a picture for illustration. "It comprises the labia majora or the outer fold, the labia minora or the inner fold, the urethra, and the clitoris. The clitoris alone has thousands of nerve endings, maybe eight thousand. When stimulated, the nerves signal the brain to increase blood flow to the pelvic region, which then causes swelling and secretion of fluid in the vulva and vagina canal for easy penetration during sexual intercourse. In short, the clitoris makes a woman want to have sex because of the pleasure it generates. In the circumcised female, they cut off the clitoris. This results in no signal to the brain, and no desire. It's the opposite effect of male circumcision."

The Osunih looked confused. "Amah," he called Candice. "Can you explain what Brea just said about the woman's circumcision? I really don't understand all these grammas."

"Brea said," Candice paused, thinking of the best way to clarify what Brea explained to them. "Papa, when you want to eat fufu or pounded yam, you eat it with soup, right?"

"Yes, melon soup, draw soup or banga soup."

"Okay, imagine if there is no soup. How would the fufu or pounded yam feel in your mouth?"

"It would be dry and hard to swallow."

"Unless you want to eat corn instead."

"No!" the Osunih bellowed. "That's light food for entertainment. A proper meal is fufu or pounded yam with soup and assorted meat."

"Good. Papa let's say you're hungry and waiting. You find out that there is no soup to eat your fufu because they killed the mama who cooks the soup." Her eyes met Babza's. He gave her a questioning look. She raised her hand lightly and nodded her head to show she knew what she's doing. "Papa, how would you feel?"

"Very upset. That means I can't eat my fufu."

"Good. Brea just told us that the clitoris," she pointed to it in the picture. "has something inside it that helps in enjoying sex." Thinking in a man's language, she said, "In your car, you need engine oil or lubricant to allow all the moving parts inside the engine to rub against each other smoothly and not overheat or wear out, right?"

"Yes," the Osunih responded.

"In the woman's body, the clitoris helps to make the oil or lubricant that prepares the vagina for the man to come inside her easily with no trouble. The lubricant prevents dryness, so that their skin can rub against each other

76

smoothly with no pain or wahala." She saw the lift on Babza's face. "The clitoris is like the mama that cooks the soup for your fufu. In female circumcision, they cut off the clitoris, which means they cut off mama's head."

"Ahh!" Farakhi screeched.

Babza added sadly, but with a witty undertone, "And when the mama dies and no soup, we men have to force ourselves to swallow balls of fufu, if we don't choke first."

The men chuckled.

Candice suddenly jumped to her feet, and then pulled Babza by his hand to the kitchen. "We will be right back," she announced. She gently closed the door behind them. "I don't know if I should share this. Some people would disagree with Brea that removing the man's foreskin is good for his sexual pleasure."

"What do you mean?"

"The uncircumcised men say the foreskin has nerve endings, too. They get intense pleasure from gliding the foreskin back and forth over the rim. That is how most of them masturbate."

"You this woman," Babza screeched in amazement. "How do you know these things?"

"I ask a lot of questions," Candice uttered effortlessly.

"I won't know about that."

"On a second thought, maybe I shouldn't share it."

"Is that it?" Babza had a grin on his face.

"Yes."

"Let's get back there."

They reentered the room

"Sorry. We're back," Babza said.

Soon as they sat down, Candice turned her attention to the men of God. "What do you think of masturbation?" She glanced at Babza. "Sorry, I have to ask."

Pastor Odio took on the question. "The wasting of semen is unacceptable in God's book."

Babza pulled everyone to the question at hand. "Back to Satan. Now let's apply the strategies he used on Eve and Jesus to the people in the time of Abraham or his descendants. Let's come up with the questions or statements that Satan could have used to convince them to circumcise the females."

"I have a suggestion," Father Jacobs said. "Let's use Eve's encounter. Her case was like that of the people of Abraham. They were simple human beings. Jesus was both man and God, he knew the full power of temptation."

"I agree," Pastor Odio said.

Babza had no objection to the suggestion. "We will do it this way. Everyone, get a piece of paper and pen. Write how you think Satan did it. We will compare answers and pick the most popular ones. Brea, please give everyone a paper and pen from my father's table there." He pointed to the table.

Brea distributed the papers and pens. They got to work. After a long-drawn-out silence, Babza asked if they have finished the assignment.

They said, yes.

Turning to Brea and Candice, Babza directed them to collect the answers and sort them according to each strategy. He announced the results.

"Strategy Number 1: Did God really say only males should be circumcised? Are you sure he didn't include females in the covenant?

Strategy number 2: God said the uncircumcised will not be among his people. You will lose your uncircumcised wives and daughters. Circumcise your females so they can remain with you.

Strategy number 3: Remember how Pharoah took Abraham's wife in Egypt. Protect what is yours, you must circumcise your females to keep them faithful to you. You lock your valuables inside your house so that others won't steal them. You must also do the same with your beautiful wives and daughters, lock up their vagina so that other men won't have sex with them. Remove the exposed part of their vagina and stitch the remaining parts together to preserve their purity and virginity."

Babza looked around for any comment, none came from the floor. "Do we all come to an agreement with the questions and statements that Satan may have used to convince the people?"

A resounding 'yes' rose from the floor.

"Looking at this from a business perspective," Babza continued. "Satan is an equal opportunity employer. Regarding the slave traders who were foreigners, using the same techniques, Satan would have said to them:

1. Didn't you hear that God told your business partners, Abraham, and his people to circumcise everyone, including your female slaves?

2.   God said anyone who is not circumcised will not be among his people. They will not buy your uncircumcised female slaves. Circumcise all your slaves, male and female, if you want to trade with them.

3.   You deserve to be as wealthy as Abraham and his people. Circumcised female slaves will earn you higher profit. Remove everything between her legs and sew her up to show her purity and virginity. It will prevent her from prostituting herself among her fellow slaves and other slave owners. A circumcised female will be faithful and obedient to her master. You will gain more wealth."

"Good thinking," Candice commended him.

Babza thanked everyone for staying through the task. Making a closing summation, he said, "In the past few days, I got to know this fallen angel, Satan. He despises authority, one of the reasons he rebelled against God. He is a master of deception who is full of arrogance and slander. He makes up his own messages and secretly introduces them to us in destructive deviations that go against God's words. He promises freedom from what has held us captive while making us a slave to the bad habits we have mastered. An expert in greed and adultery, he appeals to our lustful and sinful nature, enticing us to live in error. Like an expert fisher that uses a bait to lure a fish into his net, Satan looks for what we want to hear, especially things that appeal to our ego and then uses them to hook us, holding us captive.

It's no accident that at the time God told Abraham that he will be the father of many descendants, God also told him to circumcise all males in his household. God refined the tool that men will use to do the job of procreation."

"Uh, hum," the Osunih interrupted. "A farmer has to sharpen the hoe he uses to dig the ground so he could harvest more crops."

"Well said," Chief Tabor remarked.

Candice joined in, "Whatever God put in place; Satan has his own plan. He knew that a damaged female sexual organ would discourage the man from mating with her. He might even reject her completely."

Pastor Odio interjected. He turned to Father Jacobs, "Remember what Jesus told the men who were telling him that Moses allowed them to divorce the woman." Father Jacobs nodded. "Jesus told them Moses allowed divorce because they were hard-hearted. Now, this is making sense. They may have been doing this thing even before Moses' time."

"Yes," Father Jacobs responded. "The women were probably so badly damaged that the men maltreated them. Moses had to tell them to set her free. Jesus said it wasn't so in the beginning. In the beginning, Adam loved Eve. They were naked and not ashamed."

"Makes sense," Candice replied. "Female circumcision can result in infection that can cause damages to the tissues in her vulva and may lead to Vaginal Fistula. She may smell because of urine leakages."

"Smell?" Farakhi shrieked. "This is not good at all."

"Hah," grunted Chief Tabor. "I didn't know this Satan is this wicked."

Father Jacobs spoke, "The men, too, were wicked. In Luke 13: 10-17, Jesus healed a woman on a Sabbath day, and the synagogue leader admonished Jesus. Jesus called him a hypocrite who unties his donkey from the stall on Sabbath, but would not let the woman, daughter of

Abraham whom Satan has tied down for eighteen years, be set free from her bondage."

"People have evil in them since the beginning of time," Pastor Odio commented. "In Amos 5:14, the Lord told the people if they want to live, they must stop doing wrong and do good." He raised his voice a pitch. "A synagogue leader is supposed to set good example. God sent several prophets to the people, but their hearts were so hard and full of wickedness. God is patient and generous, he had to send his own son to show us the way."

"The synagogue leader valued an animal more than the woman," Candice said sadly, and then continued, "To promote female circumcision, Satan blindfolds us by spreading fabrications. His followers propagate lies, saying the clitoris is toxic, it can kill a baby if the fetus's head touches it during childbirth. They claim female circumcision is a rite of passage, it improves hygiene, ensures virginity, prevents promiscuity and infidelity. These lies have sustained the practice around the world, killing millions of girls, and left permanent damages on those who survive.

United Nations data estimates two hundred million women and girls alive today have been circumcised, and the number is growing. The actual number may run into billions because the procedure is done mainly in private homes, in rural and the most remote villages. It is done in secret, kept hush hush just the way Satan likes it. It is done on female babies as young as 7 days old to adult women. Performed by a collaboration of family members and the cutters. Who will report it and to whom? Is it the baby, family members or the cutter? To what authority, law enforcement, village head, or religious leaders?

Infibulation, the most severe type, is popular in the countries around the Horn of Africa, which I think it's because they are closest to the origin, the land around the Euphrates and Egypt. The severity reduces the further you move away from the source. The practice has spread to other regions through greedy slave traders and the migration of believers." She took a swig of water.

Brea raised her hand to get Candice's attention. "I heard that some men favor the infibulation type because it makes the entrance to the vagina canal small, which heightens their sexual pleasure during penetration."

Candice cringed with disgust. "Yes. The practicing societies favor it because it appeals to the man's ego. Satan knows that once he inflates the man's ego, the woman would submit accordingly no matter how irrational he reasons. We find out that mothers are the ones who take their daughters to the house of butchery.

The practicing communities don't question the origin because the 'supposed' benefits outweigh man's desire to discern the hidden truth or he fears that what he'd discover may not advance his egoistic existence, so it is easier to call it tradition or custom."

Holding herself straight and speaking with conviction, Candice added, "God will never cause this much damage to his beloved daughters. He created her to be a helpmate, to bring forth babies through this amazing sexual organ. God has no reason to hurt women. Only Satan has a motive, strong enough to reign havoc on billion daughters of the earth."

She ran out of breath and sat down.

Babza walked up to her and lightly parted her on her shoulder and then returned to his chair.

"This looks bad," Pastor Odio said. "In 1 Corinthians 12:24, God put our bodies together in such a way that even the parts that are least important are valuable. He did this to make all parts of the body work together smoothly, with each part caring about the others. If one part of our body hurts, we hurt all over. If one part of our body is honored, the whole body will be happy."

"You're right," Babza acknowledged the scripture verse. "If God wanted the circumcision of females, he would have said so. As Brea explained, all parts of the female's sexual organ have a purpose. God didn't make a mistake, he put every anatomical structure in place for a reason.

God introduced male circumcision for a good purpose, but Satan saw an opportunity for his evil schemes. In female circumcision, he killed two birds with one stone. Mutilation of the woman's genitals would reduce the propensity of her getting pregnant, hindering population growth. It would also lower the risk of her producing the offspring that would crush him.

We heard earlier that a third of heavenly angels followed him. He must be very charming and persuasive. He likes to walk up and down, looking for prey. Whereas God empowers us to use our free will to think and act with love, Satan acts like a hands-on manager who is active in his captives' lives, coaching and interacting with them until he destroys them.

The people that came after the flood, the descendants of Noah, were obviously a young generation. They predated Christianity and Islamic religion. They were naïve and ignorant of the true nature of God and no match for Satan who has hundreds of years of experience in manipulation.

His techniques worked on Eve and Adam. Why not use it again? Satan took advantage of them and introduced female circumcision which was contrary to God's command. For centuries, despite the trauma, the short and long-term health damages that circumcision has caused our women and girls, the practice is kept alive by lies as narrated earlier.

Female circumcision was a windfall for those foreign slave traders. They must have gulped it down like thirsty men who found cold bottles of coke cola on a hot humid afternoon. Money is a great motivator. As the traders moved from place to place, buying slaves, they must have advertised the benefits of female circumcision to their suppliers, encouraging and enticing them with increased payment. Men who used to hunt for animals turned to slave hunters. Local herbalists or anyone daring enough to cut human flesh found another source of income. It takes a few people to perform circumcision, and everyone gets paid. Business boom!"

Chief Tabor interjected, "Son, listen to this." All eyes turned to him. "My grandfather once told me that when he was young, children would disappear, never to be seen again. These were children of the very poor in the village and wayward children. Back then, they didn't have a prison. I think they sold them to these people you're talking about."

"It's likely that the hunters kidnapped children or paid good money to poor families to give up their daughters in the pretense of finding them jobs or husbands."

With the fingers of his left hand supporting his chin, Pastor Odio raised his right hand to gain everyone's attention. "In the book of Esther, King Xerxes of Persia ruled over many provinces from India to Ethiopia. He had many parties for the important people. It was during one of those parties that his queen disobeyed him. They dethroned her and made Esther the new queen. Sometimes his parties could go on for days. They must have had plenty of servants and slaves to serve them. They had plenty of women in their harem."

"Aha!" Candice jumped in. "The merchants brought women from India. That explains why there is female circumcision in India, Pakistan, the Middle East, and all the way to West Africa."

"You need to read that book," Pastor Odio rejoined. "Those people knew how to party. Display of wealth and drunkenness."

Babza inhaled deeply before he began to speak. "My research shows that most of the female slaves were used as sex slaves. It makes sense that the men were thrilled at the idea of doing the infibulation type. Stitch her up, the tighter the better." In his mind, Babza cursed the ruthless, wild, sex hungry men. "Illegal human trafficking is a lucrative business till today."

Babza paused briefly, thinking. During lunch, his gut feeling told him there was a missing piece of the puzzle. Satan is a reactive and vengeful being. Something happened that pushed him to launch his campaign for female circumcision. What was it? He remembered Kayah's account of his experience in Somalia. The infibulation technique is so extreme, why? After lunch, he read the book of Genesis, trying to find clues. His search hovered around Lot and his daughters in Genesis 19:30. He found some pointers there. He needed to clarify some things with Candice before presenting them to the group.

He excused himself and signaled to Candice to come with him. Candice followed him to the kitchen.

"Do women masturbate?" he asked her.

Candice was thrown off. Her chest pushed up. She threw her head back, blinking her eyes.

"Why are you looking like that? Answer the question."

"Give me a minute to compose myself," she mumbled.

"How come you had no problem talking about male masturbation and now you look shocked?"

"Why do you ask?"

"Answer the question first. Something has been bothering me about that infibulation technique."

She inhaled deeply before saying, "Women don't tell each other these things." Her eyes met his gaze, and then she turned away.

"I'm not looking to make a judgment on anyone," he said softly. "I'll tell you in a minute what I'm thinking."

Facing him, she said bluntly, "This is another area where men and women are different. Orgasm for a man produces ejaculation of sperm, orgasm for a woman does not release her egg. I don't know what to say."

"You said men use their foreskin to induce masturbation, right?"

"Yes."

"Answer this, can women use their clitoris to stimulate themselves?"

"Yes."

"What was so hard to say about that?" He laughed at her coyness. "My next question is, how do you feel about snakes?"

"What?" Her face wrinkled. "I hate that thing. I run from it as fast as I can."

"How about if you find it near your child, would you run too?"

With a dreadfully loud pitch, she responded, "Hell, no!"

"You would protect your child."

"That's not even debatable. Why are you asking these strange questions?"

"You'll find out in a minute." He pulled her hand. Both walked back to the group. "Sorry, I had to confirm something from Candice," Babza apologized.

Servants brought refreshments into the room.

"That's fine, " Chief Tabor replied. "Eat something."

Babza grabbed a bottle of water and meat pie. He handed the same to Candice. The servants served the others.

Moments later, Babza shared his questions and findings. "I wanted to know what motivated Satan's campaign for female circumcision. I pondered the infibulation procedure. The technique is extreme. With no anesthetic, no sterile equipment, they cut off the clitoris, tear out the labia surfaces, use needle and thread to pierce wounded skin, and then sew them together in several places as if tying shoelaces for a football match. Why such cruelty?"

"If that was done to us men, the world would have ended by now," Farakhi said with disgust.

"It appears to be a personal vendetta," Babza summed. "A punishment for something terrible done to the one who is offended."

"There's a difference between discipline and child abuse," Candice uttered painfully, "It's so brutal."

"It's criminal," Brea added.

"Yes," Babza said. "I had to think outside the box. I looked beyond what my tour guide revealed in my vision. In Genesis 19: 30-38, I found out that Lot and his two daughters were the only ones left after the destruction of Sodom and Gomorrah. Thinking that there were no men in their world, the girls preserved their family line. They got their father drunk and had sex with him. The older one went first and the next day the younger girl had her turn. If their father was so drunk that he didn't know they were his daughters, he must be out of his senses. That means the girls masterminded the sexual act. They got pregnant and each birthed a son. Further down in Genesis 38:7-10, one brother, Onan, was instructed to have sex with his dead brother's wife to produce offspring for his brother. Whenever Onan had sex with his sister-in-law, he would spill his semen on the ground to avoid fathering an offspring. He lost his life for what he did." Babza paused a moment. He drank some water.

"Mr. Walkabout, Satan, saw all these events. He would applaud Onan for his disobedience because Onan's action aligned with his mission. His response would be different for the girls' actions. Let's inspect Lot's daughters and how Satan may have reacted.

Before the destruction of Sodom and Gomorrah, Lot had wealth. The daughters lived a luxurious life with maids and servants to serve them. They had husbands in waiting. Some rowdy men came to their house, demanding to have sex with two visitors in their household. Lot offered the girls to be raped by a herd of men. Luckily, they were spared. While running away from disaster, they lost their mother, who turned into a pillar of salt. Except for their father, everything they have perished. Their lives turned 360 degrees. They ended in isolation, living in a cave with one man. Under these circumstances, most of us would wallow in self-pity, cry woe-is-me, harbor bitterness, anger, fear, or even sink into depression. The girls didn't do any of these. Instead, they confronted the realities of their world. They knew that the linage of Lot depended on them. Rather than complain, they sacrificed their emotional complexes and focused on their purpose. They rose above all the negative forces to produce offspring.

"This is interesting," Brea uttered. She leaned forward to hear how this would unfold.

"After the fall in the garden of Eden, God put enmity between the serpent and the woman. It is no mistake that the next phrase was about their offspring. For her child, a rational mother would never agree with Satan."

"God's words are sharper than a double-edge sword," Pastor Odio commented.

Babza nodded his head. "Pastor, thank you for saying that. Once again, Satan wanted to mock God's words. He plotted to overrule the enmity that God put between the woman and him. By inserting disasters into the lives of Lot's daughters, he created a hostile environment, hoping that their negative experiences would cripple them emotionally. He thought bullying them would make them fall into his traps. Staying true to God's words, the girls distanced themselves from Satan by refusing to succumb to his influence on their lives." Turning to Father Jacobs, Babza said, "The girls overcame the interrogation of temptation to sink into despair."

Father Jacobs nodded in agreement. "Very true."

Babza resumed, "The girls maintained the protective shield that God decreed when he put a wall between the woman and the serpent. The Lot girls aligned themselves with God's words. They remained positive, think clearly, and proactively plan, using the available resources. Hmm," Babza grunted. Cracking a joke, he said, "Satan is looking like a fool right now."

There was laughter from the group.

"Satan can't read minds," Babza continued. "He can't take away one's free will. He didn't think the two virgins would get their father drunk and get pregnant. Little did he know that a woman knows no bounds when it comes to the fruit of her womb. She would sacrifice her very soul for her child. Through their sacrificial love for the family, the Lot girls dug into their natural maternal intuition. They applied a higher level of emotional intelligence to bring about procreation, the very thing that Satan despised. The girls proved to Satan that when action is motivated by love, human beings are resilient. They are conquerors. The girls beat him at his games, humiliating him. This was personal, he had to revenge."

All eyes were on Babza. They stared at him, speechless.

"Satan is vengeful. We said earlier, he wants to be like God. He wants to do anything that God does. In the fight for the seed, he witnessed Onan lose his life for spilling his seed on the ground. The Lord was displeased at Onan's action, and he was killed. Satan was displeased at the girls' actions, so they, too should be killed. Could he kill the girls? Only God has the power to take a life because he created the life. Satan knows he can't take life, but he can manipulate a situation to put lives at risk. His revenge on the girls would be to endanger all women through the

91

organ that the girls used to embarrass him. Through circumcision, Satan used his powers of influence to cause others to damage as many girls as possible with the intent to kill them."

"Lord almighty!" Father Jacobs exclaimed. Reflectively he said, "Jesus told us in John 10:10,' the thief comes to steal and kill and destroy.'"

Candice screeched, "This is madness!" She stood up. Shaking her hands, she threw punches into the air. "Satan, you're a loser, stupid idiot, foolish copycat, you will die in hell."

Speaking fiercely, Brea joined, "Even in my generation, Satan influences how society treats women." She stood up, highly agitated. "In politics, religion, education, or social gathering, they relegate us down. Satan, I rebuke you!"

"From the day God created Eve, his hatred for women never stops," Candice retorted. "He wants to kill us."

"What kind of wahala is this?" the Osunih asked. "Why did God create this Satan?"

"I wonder o…," Chief Tabor threw in. "If God goes one way, Satan will go the other way. What does one do to a child that does not listen to his elders?"

"This one pass me," Farakhi voiced his bafflement.

Father Jacobs muttered to himself, "Romans 8:28, in all things, God works for the good of those who love him, who have been called according to his purpose." He called Candice and Brea's attention. "Trust in God. Another virgin was obedient to God, and she bore a savior that would save the world. Mary, the mother of Jesus, could have been frightened when the angel told her she would be pregnant, but she was brave and trusted God."

"Satan doesn't have the last word," Pastor Odio joined in calmly. "Jesus elevated women throughout his ministry. Even though what the Lot girls did appeared sinful in our eyes, their actions produced the offspring that led to the lineage of Ruth to King David and the messiah."

"Pastor," Farakhi called. "Satan expected the girls to sit in the cave, crying that the enemy did this to them. They would have died still complaining. Despite all the disasters, they were strong. This shows that the girls were smarter than the master of deception." He turned to Candice and Brea. "You're very special to God."

Babza walked to the ladies, curbed their shoulders with his arms, and sat them down. "Don't take this personal," he said coolly to them. "The reason for this exercise is to get a better understanding." He turned to everyone. "Why do doctors ask us for our health history when we go to the hospital? They ask to enable them to gain a comprehensive insight into our illness. It's important to know the origin of the disease and the progression to diagnose the problem and find solutions. I realize it's been a long day. We're almost done."

"Satan cannot touch you, ladies," Pastor Odio threw in. "In Romans 8:38, we're told that nothing can separate us from the love of God."

Babza hurried up to finish his summation. "How did the practice become a tradition?" He redirected everyone's attention. "Eventually, everything must end. The boom of the slave trade probably ended when men discovered other natural resources that fetched higher returns. The local slave hunters may have kept the practice going, unaware that the trade itself has lost its momentum. By the time they realized the trade has ended, the practice of female circumcision has taken root and continued to be propagated by the lies that supported it. Do you think the people who brought the idea to these local hunters came back to stop them?" No one responded. Babza furnished the answer. "Of course not, they have other ventures and new partners with whom to party. As Candice mentioned earlier, it suited the men's egos. They called it tradition or customs, the new norm. Despite the number of deaths from excessive bleeding or infection, lifelong trauma, infertility, and other adverse health issues, the practice continues. And for centuries, they have held us hostage with lies. Satan is celebrating."

"Ha, to think in this very village we kept doing it for many years," Farakhi uttered sadly. He turned to Candice. "Thank you for opening our eyes when you fought for Bekyah."

"We didn't know any of these," the Osunih added.

"Thank you," Candice responded.

All eyes returned to Babza.

"Apart from refining the man's sexual organ, God also removed the curse he had put on the ground when Adam sinned. The ground became easier for man to cultivate and produce wealth. Male circumcision was a game-changer for the man; he had a heightened libido and wealth to make as many children as he desired. The result of God's covenant was population growth? You can see that God included the slaves, too. He excluded no one from his desire to populate the earth. Satan devised his own plans to counter that growth. He used God's words to orchestrate his evil plans. By hijacking female sexuality, he held all of us in bondage.

Misery loves company; they have kicked Satan out of heaven, he wants many of us to be with him in hell. He is relentless, he wants to make those practicing female circumcision commit sin against God.

Pastor Odio turned to Father Jacobs and whispered something to him. They both got up. "It's our turn to talk with each other," he said lightly to the group. "Excuse us for a minute."

They headed to the kitchen.

Pastor Odio stretched his arms before speaking. "I want to share with you what I found so insightful in Babza's vision. It began with the beginning of creation to the end."

"What do you mean?"

"The last part of Babza's vision was the woman whose child the dragon waited to devour him. The dragon failed; it was defeated."

"Yes."

"The child represents Jesus Christ."

Awareness dawned on Father Jacobs. His eyebrow lifted. "It makes sense. It explains the inclusion in his vision."

"I think it was a message of hope. Whereas Adam's disobedience led to man's separation from the spirit of God, Jesus leads us back to God."

"And when we reunite with God, there will be no more pain."

Pastor Odio smiled, nodding his head. "I gained a deeper understanding from these discussions."

Father Jacobs nodded in agreement. "Me, too."

"The prayer Jesus taught us reflects everything we covered."

95

"The Lord's prayer?"

"Yes. Begin with our Father," Pastor Odio proposed. "It establishes a personal relationship. A father has the responsibility of taking care of his family and the child has access to the father."

"Hallowed be thy name, is a salutation that gives reverence and honor to the Father, our creator," Father Jacobs said.

"Thy kingdom come, this is what Jesus brought to us, faith, hope, and love," Pastor Odio uttered. "It's a reminder that at the end of our trials and tribulations, we shall be in God's kingdom. Jesus will come again to gather his faithful. Through him, we will reunite with God."

"Thy will be done on earth as it is in heaven." Father Jacobs explained. "God wants us to share in his eternal glory at the end of our time. To do that, we must partake in his will on earth. Our lives should be about denying our egotistic selves, and in humility, aligning ourselves with God's purpose. In heaven, God has assigned each of us a task. On earth, we must discover and accomplish the task that was assigned to us."

"Give us this day our daily bread," Pastor Odio stated. "We pray for physical and spiritual food. We need a daily dose of a healthy diet, exercise, and words from the scripture as ammunition to fight the evil one. We should study God's words and know how to apply them to our lives. Otherwise, Satan will confuse us."

"Forgive us our trespasses as we forgive those who trespass against us," Father Jacobs said. "In forgiveness, we submit to God, who does not look at our deficiencies but frees us to live in love and peace. In unforgiveness, we become hard-hearted, we submit to Satan, who leads us to his dominion to destroy us."

"Lead us not into temptation," Father Jacobs continued. "This is recognizing that we cannot do it alone. We need God's help to overcome the interrogation of temptation."

"But deliver us from the evil one," Pastor Odio finished. "We recognize that there is a spiritual warfare out there. The enemy is walking around, looking for who to devour. We should be aware of him, understand his techniques, and seek God's counsel to protect ourselves. We should stay connected with the Holy Spirit to guide and direct us in making the right decisions."

"That's a good breakdown of the Lord's prayer." Father Jacobs smiled.

"Let's get back to the group."

They returned to the living room. They shared their thoughts with the group.

"Interesting. Jesus covered everything in that prayer." Chief Tabor acknowledged the breakdown.

"Yes," Pastor Odio replied. "That is why he said in John 10:10, 'He came so that we can have a life of abundance.'"

Babza thanked the men of God. "Thank you for that insight." He rounded up the discussions. "In the beginning, God made man in his image and gave him dominion over all he created. When man was alone, God created a helper, the woman. She was the height of God's creative excellence. Satan knows that wounding her would cause sadness for men, and God. As it was in the beginning, we men will protect our women. We have unmasked the culprit so that female circumcision will never again hurt any girl or woman. God imprinted his very nature in us, to love and care for each other. Satan, in his war against God, uses us as a pun. We will stand up for God. Like David, who used stones to defeat Goliath for speaking against God, we will turn the razor from our females to where it really belongs; to Satan, the greatest HIJACKER."

A sigh of relief swept the room. Slouching shoulders and arms dropped over arms of their chairs. They looked exhausted.

"Our job is done," Chief Tabor announced. "Let's have some food."

A variety of dishes and drinks waited on the dinner table. Their conversations drowned the tension in the air as they walked to the dining room. They sat down to eat.

Chapter 14

Babza walked into Candice's compound to meet a birthday party for her father in full swing. The audience of many children, women, and men sang a happy birthday song to him. Current music came on and they danced. He watched Candice twirl around the dancers. She moved with the smoothness of an athlete, her body curving with the musical beats. Her movement put a smile on his face. She caught him looking at her and came forward.

Smiling broadly, she asked, "How long have you been here?"

"Long enough to see you, charming everyone."

She stole a quick glance at her father. "I'm so glad to see him having fun. "

"Just left my father in a good mood. It's his birthday, too."

"I wonder about that coincidence."

"Why?"

"You and I keep crossing paths. It was a tiny baby on our way to school when we were young. Then you were here to help me in saving Bekyah, and we came back here to fish out the truth. Our parents sharing the same birthday in the same village tell me this was all planned."

"Hmm."

"We're characters in somebody else's play. They determine when and where our characters show up in the big stage called life."

"Can we sit down? I have a question to ask you."

She pulled him to the side, away from the noise. "Regarding how you feel about me. We had this conversation years ago. I'm a middle-aged woman. I have nothing to offer you like these young women in Nigeria."

"Hold on to that thought, that's not what I want to ask."

"Oh! Sorry for being presumptuous."

He laughed. "I would never look at pounded yam the same again." She laughed out loud. "How did you come up with that analogy?"

"I don't know. My brain is wired for quick thinking."

"I like this brain of yours. One never knows what would pop out of it."

They both laughed.

"Anyway, my question is, using your analogy, when the mama's head is cut off, how then do you make the woman enjoy sex?"

"Hmm," Candice sigh deeply. "We need to sit down."

They sat on an empty set of chairs nearby. Candice pulled a table and smoothened a piece of napkin on it. "Do you have a pen?" He searched his pockets and found none. She called someone to bring her handbag. "I want to show you how mama is built. I think it would make things clearer."

"You told me you're a visual person. I have to remember to carry a paper and pen when I come around you."

"Not all the time." She chuckled. "Only when you hit me with a serious question like this. While we wait, know that every woman is different. What one woman enjoys may differ from what another enjoys. The mama they cut off has a high concentration of nerve endings. There are other areas with nerve endings, like the nipple. You both have to play around to find what makes her feel good."

"Suppose she's not the playing around type?"

"Everybody has what gladdens their soul. I said soul, not eyes. Something that they innately respond to with a smile. Our subconscious self is always searching for something we love, things like friendliness, laughter, understanding, kindness, support, sharing, and respect. Everything starts with what we feed the brain and what messages the brain then sends to the rest of the body. The most important thing is to enjoy each other's company and not look at sex as if it's food that we would die if we don't have it. All women, including the not playing-around type, like the things I mentioned even if they don't verbalize it. You both should be open to an objective conversation." She fixed her eyes on him. "Communicate!" The maid gave her a handbag. She pulled out a paper and pen.

He held her hand, stopping her from writing on the paper. "Is that what you do?" He saw the puzzled look on her face. "I mean what do you like?"

She hesitated before giving him an answer. She wanted to say, it's none of your business, but her rascally mind wanted to play with his head. "Well," she drawled. "I like to soak in a jacuzzi with warm bubbling water first. Then,

101

when I come out of the water, he would rub lotion all over my body to moisturize my skin and keep it soft." She saw his face from the corners of her eyes, he was staring at her. "I like nice fragrance in the room, so it's necessary to have some scented candles burning. I also like a little dance." She laid more emphasis on the next statement. "Yes, he has to like dancing as part of the process." She stopped talking, waiting for his reaction. No response came from him. She got irritated, what use is trying to annoy someone and get no response. She quickly added, "I do the dancing, sometimes I do yoga or exercise to relax my muscles." In a snappy tone she said loudly, "Why are we talking about me?" She slapped the paper on the table and drew.

She drew a shape like an upside-down cone. Pointing to the cone, she said, "This is mama, there is a gland inside her, under the prepuce, the skin. Even when they cut off the head or part of the body of mama, the remaining part is buried under the skin, inside the woman's pubic bone. The activation rate depends on how much was cut off. In total removal, you should massage that area to wake things up. Are you following me so far?"

"Yes, keep going."

"You will need some lubricant to assist in the massaging, not Vaseline, too heavy. Don't use palm oil, groundnut oil, or any other household oil. They sell lubricants in the pharmacy or chemist."

"Hum," Babza exhaled.

"What?" She saw a frown on his face. "You asked!"

"What would she be doing while I'm trying to wake up this hidden treasure?"

"That's why I told you to communicate with each other. She can actually start it before you come to bed."

"That's good to know."

"Another thing is positions. When she's on top, the angle of mama meeting papa puts more pressure on mama to wake up."

"Ah, I like that even better."

"Again, be open to each other and explore. It's your bodies, in your private home, no shame."

"Thank you. I feel a lot better."

"You're welcome."

"Now to my real question. I asked you to marry me years ago, you didn't give me an answer." He stopped her when she opened her mouth to speak. "I'm a middle-aged man, too. Our people say, what an adult can see sitting down, a child cannot see it even if they climb a ladder."

"Meaning?"

"Age and experience are packed with wisdom, wittiness, laughter, less stress, and lots of relaxation. Young people are still trying to figure out their lives. Why would I want to interrupt their path to self-discovery? They can do that with young men their age. So, princess, don't give me that talk about all the young women in Nigeria. The youthfulness and energy in you are unparallel, you're my baby for life."

She saw her father coming in their direction. "Here's my father." They both got up to meet with him. The Osunih pulled Candice off to meet some of the new arrivals.

Chapter 15

At the local airport, Babza gazed at a plane docked on the runway. It reminded him she'd be on her way back to America soon. He knew he had better move fast. She was an independent and accomplished woman. Why would she want to remarry? Her disastrous marriage must have left an indelible mark on her heart. There's a high possibility that she'd never trust another man again. That could be her reason for refusing his offer. He knew he'd rather be with her than any other woman. He liked her quick thinking. Whereas he felt restrained in expressing his thoughts, she had no qualms in showing her zestful energy in living. She has a sharp intuition, which he liked.

Yes, he would marry her. They'd make a good life together. She wasn't egotistic about herself, which is admirable. He has heard about complementary characters; it took knowing her to know the meaning. It amazed him at how she knew how to push him. She took him to a level that was grander than if he had done it alone. Together, they produced an improved result. They didn't have to say it, they just knew where to take it to make it better. Between them, there's no competition, but a sweet harmonious completion.

He had wondered about sex with her. How would he satisfy her? Thanks to the conversation with her, he has confidence it would be great. He'd ask her again to marry him. A slight jitter went through him, he shut it off. He knew he was on the right path.

While he waited for her, he called his friend, Kayah, to tell him about their discovery on female circumcision. With both their professional skills, they resolved to share the discovery with the rest of the world. It would be a daunting task; their efforts would be worth it. He saw Candice enter the departure hall.

"Princess Amah," he said when he neared her.

"Prince Babza," she returned.

"You were fantastic in the village. Your kinsfolks love you."

"Yes, thank you." She smiled brightly.

"I spoke with my friend, Kayah. He said his sister is with him in Lagos. She's doing fine."

"So glad to hear that."

"Kayah and I decided to use our skills, my advertising business and his journalism, to spread awareness and debunk the beliefs that have kept the practice alive for so long."

"That sounds like a good idea. I think people need to know the genesis of female circumcision. Understanding its origin will help to eradicate it completely and bring healing to the millions who have been affected by the procedure."

Staring at her, he said, "Will you marry me?"

"We had this conversation years ago."

"And you didn't give me an answer. None of us is leaving until you give me one."

She glared at him for a long time, thinking. She heard an announcement of their flight on the PA system and took off. He shuttled behind her. She was fast.

"Stop her!" he yelled out, drawing other passengers' attention.

One of the two younger men close by Babza said, "Bros, we'll go after her. She will return whatever she stole from you." The men ran after Candice. They reached her and held her until Babza caught up with them.

"Let me go!" Candice roared at the young men. She struggled to remove their hold on her.

"Don't release her," Babza instructed the men. "She owes me."

"Prince, the answer is, yes."

"She said, yes," Babza announced to the crowd. "She will be my wife."

The young men quickly let go of her arms.

The spectators clapped their hands, cheering them on.

Conclusion

As it was in the beginning, so will it be in the end. Through grace, man and woman will be glorified with their creator, the God of the universe.

Matthew 7:7-8 (NIV)
"Ask and it will be given to you; seek and you will find; knock and the door will be opened to you. For everyone who asks receives; the one who seeks finds; and to the one who knocks, the door will be opened."

The writing of this book

The Greatest Hijack was written in two weeks. I had no intention of writing a sequel to Saving Bekyah-Confronting Female Circumcision, Sexuality and Womanhood. I was led to it by powers beyond me.

Saving Bekyah was written in 2007, self-published it in 2008. In 2010, I traveled on a Greyhound bus from Penn Station, NJ to Newport News, Virginia to see Ellen Sudderth who conducted a book club at her house. I sold four books. I returned home with aches and pains from the long bus ride and dragged a suitcase filled with dozens of unsold books. It was too much trouble, 'wahala' as my people would say. Even though the book had great potential for a large readership, I had no time to pursue the marketing avenues. I had a demanding job as a court executive. I stored the books in my garage, gave away to interested readers and donated some to universities in Nigeria.

In June 2021, Ellen Sudderth tracked me down on Facebook; she found copies of Saving Bekyah that I left with her in 2010. She informed me she now does book discussions with authors on Facebook interfaced with Zoom. We set August 24, 2021, for an interview. I had to read the book to refresh my memory. In a conversation with Ellen shortly after the interview, I mentioned we did not discuss a chapter in the book in which I talked about

The Greatest Hijack

God's perspective on female circumcision. We set up a second interview for September 23, 2021.

Immediately after the interview, a cloud engulfed me. My spirit was thrown into confusion, I didn't know what was happening to me. I walked around in a daze; my bubbling self was gone. Friends were worried about me. I was at crossroads and lost. I prayed fervently. Then one day as I walked alone in a park, I heard a voice in my head say, write a book, call it the greatest hijack. I ran home, pulled out my laptop, and typed.

The questions came first, who, why, where, and how? In two weeks, all the answers unfolded. It turned out that all I needed to write this book were already waiting for the appointed time. Those that weren't waiting were quickly revealed through random interactions with friends, doctors, radio broadcasts, YouTube videos, and church sermons.

To God be the glory!

References:

1. Saving Bekyah Confronting Female Circumcision, Sexuality and Womanhood by Caroline Omoifo
2. Extreme Faith Bible, American Bible Society, Contemporary English version
3. The Journey, A Bible for Seeking God & Understanding Life, New International Version
4. Holy Bible, Catholic Version Good Counsel Publishing Company, Chicago Illinois
5. Saint Augustine, City of God, Penguin Classics
6. The Discernment of Spirits, An Ignatian Guide for Everyday Living, Timothy M. Gallagher, O.M.V.
7. Knowing God, J.I. Packer
8. Dr. Henry Cloud, Integrity-The Courage to Meet the Demands of Reality
9. Jesus, CEO, Using Ancient Wisdom for Visionary Leadership by Laurie Beth Jones
10. Unlocking the Bible, Pastor Collin Smith, AM 570 Radio Broadcasts
11. Explaining the Faith, Fr. Chris Alar, MIC, National Shine of Divine Mercy Chapel, Stockbridge, MA. YouTube Channel
12. UNICEF Website Data 2021

About the author

Nigerian-born Caroline Omoifo Ilogienboh was educated in Edmonton, Alberta, Canada. She lives in New Jersey, USA, where she worked in the school and court systems.

Her passion is in writing stories in which fictional characters tackle real life issues.

She wrote a young adult trilogy; Jayda's Story- Lost at the Crossroads, The Return of Tyreek, and Nowhere to Hide. Other books include, I Heard Your Call- A Collection of Poetry in Remembrance of September 11, Hatcher's Room-Men Only, Saving Bekyah –Confronting Female Circumcision, Sexuality and Womanhood, and Finding God in Small places. The Greatest Hijack is a sequel to Saving Bekyah.

Her desire to see the end of female circumcision/genital mutilation/cutting (FGM) motivated her to search for the origin and the motive for instituting the practice. It is hoped that the information shared in this book will bring healing to survivors, and a complete eradication of the procedure in practicing communities.

Caroline is a motivational speaker on spiritual enrichment for those searching for self and living an authentic life.